Memories That Never Fade

Katrena Gillis

THIS BOOK IS A WORK OF FICTION. NAMES, CHARACTERS, LOCATIONS AND EVENTS ARE EITHER A PRODUCT OF THE AUTHOR'S IMAGINATION, FICTITIOUS OR USED FICTITIOUSLY.
ANY RESEMBLANCE TO ANY EVENT, LOCALE OR PERSON, LIVING OR DEAD, IS PURELY COINCIDENTAL.

Memories That Never Fade

First edition, 2022

Memories That Never Fade

Thank you Fabian,
for being my inspiration. You gave me faith to believe in myself again.

And to my 'wifey' for all the support.

1

In order to tell you my story, first I need to tell you, Cheyenne and Sebastian's story.

~~~~ ***Prologue*** ~~~~

Cheyenne checked her appearance in the mirror before she headed to the door. Her blonde, curly hair hung to her shoulders. She wished she would have put on some sort of make-up besides eyeliner. She was pleased that the eyeliner made her green eyes look more like a brochure advertising for the waters of the Caribbean Islands. She unlocked the door to the hotel room. He was dressed in casual attire, a faded-green hoodie with worn-out, light-blue jeans. The tightness of his jeans made his ass look firm as he walked through the door.

She had always thought that Sebastian was a good-looking man. He was about 5'11" and handsome, with black hair that was almost more gray than black. He walked toward the bed and sat on the edge of the corner and peered out at the city below. She followed behind him, taking a seat on the same side of the bed.

While resting one foot behind him, she was careful to touch him only slightly. Her other foot dangled off the bed, and she nervously painted shapes and letters with her toe. He appeared nervous as he made it clear to her that he just wanted to hang out, and that was it.

"Would you like a drink?" Cheyenne asked. "I got some beer."

"Yes, that would be good." Sebastian paused a moment and then took
~~~~

a drink of the beer she had handed him. “Sarah doesn't know that I am here.”

“I won’t say anything to her, Sebastian. No one will know.” They both sat there listening to music and talking about songs they both liked, contemplating bad decisions they could be making...or are about to make. Lost in the moment, they both selected songs dear to them. Some of the songs he selected seemed chosen specifically for her, but she didn't realize it at the time. She was so caught up in the moment and mesmerized by him.

“Cheyenne, I really must be going.”

“Yes,” she stood up, pretending to allow him to leave without any form of a fight. She attempted to walk him to the door. He must have been unprepared to catch her as she stumbled into his arms, causing both of them to fall onto the bed. She stared into his blue eyes and the next thing she knew he was kissing her. With reckless abandon, she kissed him back. His kisses were rough but not unwanted. As the passion began to build, he slid his hand up her shirt. He felt around to see if the image of her breasts he had concocted in his head were all he had imagined. Suddenly he stopped as if he had hit sensory overload, and with regrettable force, he pushed away from her.

“We cannot be doing this,” Sebastian said as he stood to his feet, sounding convincing, as if he really meant it this time.

“I am fully aware that we shouldn't be doing this,” she said, reaching for his hands. He took her hands and pulled her up to him in an attempt to restrain her from moving things forward. Like a train careening off its track, he practically conceded in a loss, and then, in a victorious manner, he quickly pulled her light-purple shirt up over her head. He slid his hand down her shoulders, and the touch of his hands sent shivers up her spine. She has never done anything like this before. Well, she has, but only inside her own imagination. However, this was real. *Wait, this is real?* She had never felt the way he was making her feel in this moment. His hands made their way to her breasts. He bent down and lightly touched her nipples, fondling them with his tongue. By now her nipples are erect, and so is he. A moan escaped her lips just as he brought his lips back up to hers, thrusting his tongue into her mouth, which he thoroughly explored.

They both collapsed back onto the bed as he kissed everywhere on her chest, making sure no part was neglected. Sebastian stood again. This time leaving was no longer an option as he began unbuttoning her pants. As he slowly lifted her legs and slid them off, the only resistance were the fibers in her jeans. She now laid there in nothing but her purple-lace underwear. Her bra was halfway pushed up, revealing both of her breasts. He lightly tugged at her underwear. She thought for a moment he was going to rip them off, but instead, he was slowly and steadily pulling them down and slipping them off her. He seemed to be drinking in the moment as if it were a fine wine to be savored. He stood above her with his jeans on. Clearly, he was overdressed for this occasion. She tried to reach up to undo his belt when he pushed her back onto the bed. It became a battle of control, but Cheyenne began to plead with him, anticipating his throbbing cock. "I need you!" She knew she was practically begging him, showing him that she was devoid of any poker face.

Dropping to his knees, he let out a low, guttural growl as he ran his hands down her thighs. He suddenly wrapped his arms around her legs and pulled her to the side of the bed, almost declaring some form of ownership in a primitive way. The conquest was just beginning...he started just above her knee. Sebastian began kissing her inner thighs and slowly dragging his lips down one thigh and up the inside of the other. She could feel her ability to retain control (or lack thereof) slipping away from her as his tongue began to slip gingerly inside of her lips...unlike the lips that he had so forcefully kissed on her mouth. With these lips, he was less forceful, approaching them with the tenderness of a delicate flower – an unpollinated flower ripe for the picking.

She couldn't hold back the moans, and she stopped trying. She arched her back, lifting her hips up off the bed as he slowly nibbled on her clitoris. She wasn't completely sure what he was doing to her down there, but if she was a vault, he was cracking her code to get into her black box. With each lick, he was swiping left, swiping right, and waiting to see if he had her full approval. She whipped her head right toward him, and he knew he was pulling at every string, like a puppet master. He played her like a guitar in need of tuning. As he honed his skills, her moans became delicate cries, and she felt as if she would become hoarse from the strain on her vocal cords. And even he could not stop...he just kept lapping at her, playing her body like a fine-tuned instrument. Her body rose off the bed, and she began to think about how much control she was quickly relinquishing. "Oh my God! Please, I need you" was the cry which sealed her fate as she made her needs known, loudly and vocally. She ran her finger on top of his hair and gave a small tug. "Come here," She said with a slight quiver in her voice.

He confidently came up to settle himself on top of her, knowing he had the upper hand. "What do you want?" He mischievously and playfully asked, although just hearing it out loud is what he wanted more than anything...well, hearing that and having his dick inside her. He could taste her on his lips; she was sweet and succulent like a juicy piece of meat but one that he could devour with all his senses and keep coming back for more.

She bit her lower lip and contemplated for a moment. "You know what I want. I want you inside me." He stood up as though he were a stoic gladiator, but it was in his eyes that he couldn't, wouldn't back down. This time he wasn't even attempting to leave... he was now going to accommodate her, and just as he was reaching for the button of his jeans, she beat him to it. The button was hot. It didn't matter why it was hot; neither of them was about to heed this warning, if this was supposed to be a deterrent. There was not going to be anyone hitting the "Stop" button, and there weren't any arguments about right or wrong. What mattered was the fact that the jeans needed to be shed, like a snake that sheds its skin for new life. Welcome to the Garden of Eden, and Sabastian and Cheyenne's personal playground of ecstasy. While kissing his cheek, a sensual, gravitational pull descended over her. She began to hit sensory overload. Overcome with her desires, she explored his neck, working her way down...and even further down. Using her tongue, she continued tasting his skin. She teasingly moved her body and her tongue, convincing him with her feminine charms, running her finger over his nipples and gripping his ass with one arm. She used her free hand to unhook his belt, struggling to unhook his pants with one hand.

It was hard concentrating on what she was doing while he was kissing her neck and sliding a finger inside of her. "Mmmm ahhh," she moaned and lost more and more control over her body as cum dripped down his finger.

He pushed her down on the bed, pinning her hands slightly above her head. He started by kissing her neck, as he slowly adjusted his erect penis to perfectly line it up to slide inside her. He was absolutely no amateur with the wiles of women's bodies. His thrusts were fast and hard, as if she was to pay a toll for toying with his emotions, and he would make her pay. It wasn't long before he finished. He collapsed on top of her before he began the mumbling all over again. "This was such a mistake, and this shouldn't be happening... while he continued. He began pleading to stop and she wasn't sure if the tears he displayed were from the thought of giving into his desires or never knowing what she would taste like. As she enticed him further, he edged his way diagonally off the bed. She slightly covered his lips with her index finger as if she could silence his conscience with such a physical action. How naive of her...how naive of him. With one finger attempting to shush his mumbles she moved forward to use her powers of persuasion and began to kiss down his neck, finally making her way down to his aching cock. She slightly slid the tip in her mouth. Twirling her tongue around the slit, and with every groan she swirled her tongue more, until she finally thrusted his cock deep into her mouth.

He took her by surprise when he pulled her on his face as she continued to suck on him profusely. The pleasure was so intense that she could no longer concentrate on what she was doing to him. If this was a game, she wanted to make sure that she would be coming out on top. She decided to swing around, facing him as she climbed on top of him, and then he watched as she slipped his engorged, throbbing cock into her. He grabbed her hands with his and used her hands to pin his hands down. She felt as if she were in control, yet, she knew this act of submission by him was an act. She was completely turned on by the force he was using to hold her hands to his while pressing them into the bed. With a few movements of her hips, she collapsed on top of him, struggling to catch her breath.

And this is how my story begins......

2

Cheyenne turned on music from her playlist. She scrolled through the songs before settling on a song that fit her mood – 'Here Without You' by Three Doors Down. The words echoed around the room. *I'm here without you baby. But you're still on my lonely mind....* She stared out the window of her hotel room. This was the first time she had been away from home in so long, away from her children. Her husband told her that she needed some " me" time. Time to figure out what she wanted. If she still wanted 'us.' In all honesty, she had no idea what she wanted for sure. What Cheyenne did know is that she could not live this way anymore. Marriage is supposed to be for a lifetime. She didn't think it would feel like a life sentence. *"But what do you do when your husband is no longer the man you think about on a daily basis?"* She thought.

Her marriage had been spiraling out of control for a while – for months, or maybe years. She was not sure how long it had been since they were happy. The vows she took to promise to love her husband for the rest of her life began to feel like a lie, and now she was just going through the motions. Cheyenne could've – would've –stayed this way for quite a while, oblivious in the same manner that frogs in hot water do not jump out of the pan if the temperature is turned up to the boiling point. She was beginning to reach her very own boiling point. She is not saying that she doesn't love her husband anymore. She is just saying that she doesn't think she is still in love with him. She really can't say exactly how she feels about him anymore. He's not mean or anything toward her. He just doesn't feel that he needs to give her any attention. If Cheyenne were a flower garden and her husband the gardener, Cheyenne would have withered away a long time ago. Maybe that is what happened to the love she once had for her husband. It just withered away like anything else that gets neglected.

Most of her friends thought she was having a midlife crisis. Maybe she was, maybe she wasn't. There is one definitive thing that she knew for sure; her life as it was needed to change. She could not even begin to envision what that is or what it looks like. Everything in her life has started to spiral out of control with one single, solitary word, "Yo!"

~~~~

Cheyenne had been working for her dad for a while now. Who would've ever thought that running a car business would be so hard? She figured she would come in and take everything digital. Her father had not updated anything since her grandfather passed away two years prior, so everything was out of date. All her dad's permits had expired, and they weren't even using computers yet. She thought if she put everything on the computers and digitalized everything, she would be able to return to her simple life. But life never turns out the way you think it will.

One afternoon sticks out in her mind more vivid than any before. It was a cool day, not necessarily cold, but it was definitely tepid outside. She had to order parts. Her problem with that was the fact that she knew nothing about cars, but she also had to call the auto parts store and ask for something she knew absolutely nothing about. She got the number from her dad and began to dial.

A balancing act, so it seemed to be, she made the phone call, reluctantly asking for help from the auto parts shop. Her stance showed her frame of mind as she was sitting half on the big metal desk and half standing, watching her dad as she called. He was sitting on the chair in front of the desk, facing away from it. Her dad was a hefty, overly opinionated and well-built man who spoke few words. Standing about six-foot-six, he had ocean-blue eyes with salty-brown hair. His round face was always casting its own five-o'clock shadow. Her dad was a big old teddy bear, unless someone messed with his family. Then he could really
~~~~

get mean. She should have known that something was going to happen by the half-ass smile on her dad's face as she dialed the number. She searched her dad's face, hoping he would provide the name of the person she was supposed to ask for. To her surprise, the response on the other end would be the end of the world as she knew it.

"Yo!" came the male's voice through the other end. The man had a small accent. She was unsure what kind of accent it was or where he was from. In this part of the Midwest, it was highly unusual to hear any form of an accent. This was Iowa, after all, where they send radio announcers to in order to lose their accents. His voice was strong, yet kind.

"Excuse me?" Was the only response that she could muster, thinking and then inquiring, "What kind of way is that, to answer a business phone?"

"Well, Sugar..." He said as he paused for a moment. "I knew who was calling and 'Yo' has always worked for me before."

"It is not working anymore. I don't think that you should answer my calls like that." She was completely annoyed by the man on the other end. He may not have known it yet, but Cheyenne was bound and determined to change the way he answered the phone. "You should answer, 'Yes Ma'am' or 'Automotive Parts Unlimited, how can I help you?' Something along these lines. 'Yo', is very rude."

"Yes, Honey," was Sebastian's reply. She knew that this was going to be the hardest part of this job, trying to convince an arrogant man to not be such an ass. The way he talked to people, she doubted he had ever been taught any manners.

She gritted her teeth and asked the questions she had about the parts she needed. By the time she hung up the phone her dad was in a full, rolling laughter. "Does he always answer the phone that way?" She asked. Her dad was laughing so hard he started to hit his fist on the desk. "Dad, like really. Don't you think he is kind of rude?" By this time her dad's boisterous laughter was becoming slightly annoying. He was irritating the crap out of her. Feeling as if she was on some sort of hidden camera show like "Candid Camera" or "Practical Jokers," she rolled her eyes and retreated to the shop to get away from him. If this was a joke, it wasn't funny, at least to her. It didn't take long before her dad followed her out to the shop.

She was sitting with her feet up on the dash of her red Jeep Wrangler, TJ. She had her arms crossed, taking deep breaths. She knew that she had better get used to the way things were around here. She thought working with men had to be something akin to working with monkeys at the zoo. Although, she thought it might be easier to train monkeys to stop throwing poo easier than it would be to teach these men any manners.

"Oh, calm yourself, little one. He has answered the phone that way for as long as he has been there. We have been friends for a long time." He started to chuckle again. "And he knew you were going to be calling; I told him you were and told him to give you crap." Now her dad was rolling again with laughter.

"You're a dick, Dad, just so you know." She sat in her Jeep pouting for a little while longer before deciding to go back to the office. The rest of the day was uneventful, the same as the next few days would also be.

It was about a week later that she was sitting at her desk, working on paperwork when the phone rang. She looked down at the caller ID and saw that it was the parts store. "Skulleys, how may I help you?"

"Morning, Sweetheart! Is your daddy around?" Sebastian asked on the other end of the phone.

"Ughh, really? Yes, just a moment. I'll get him." Cheyenne replied. She got up and walked to the back shop area. "Dad, Sebastian is on the phone to talk to you."

"Hello," her dad answered. "Yup," and then he hung up.

When he finished the call, she took the phone back. It wasn't long before she was ordering parts and talking to Sebastian on a daily basis. One day she needed a part but was unsure what it was called, so she called up the parts store.

"Yo!" Sebastian's booming voice came through the telephone.

"So, I need a part and I'm not sure what it's called. It helps with cruise control. It is round and has hoses on it. It is for my Jeep."

"Send me a picture to my cell and I'll tell you what it is," he said.

"I don't have your cell number. Here is my number, 485-4948. You can just send me a message and then I will be able to send you the picture." Within a few minutes he sent her his cell number. She sent him the picture of the part. Later she found out that he did not have the part she needed.

In the few weeks since she had started working for her dad, she started talking to Sebastian almost every night when he would come to the shop. When her birthday came, she was surprised by the gift that he bought her – a part for her Jeep and paint that he had been telling her was on backorder.

"I thought it was on backorder," Cheyenne asked him with a questioning look.

"Well, it wasn't. Your dad told me your birthday was coming up." Sebastian paused for a moment and then continued. "I wanted to give it to you for your birthday."

She didn't know what to say. It had been a while since someone had gotten her something for her birthday. "Thank you," she said as she walked over and gave him a hug and kissed him on the cheek. He wrapped his left arm around her waist and embraced her in a reciprocal hug. She was unsure how long they hugged before she finally pulled away.

Looking back in her memory bank, this may have been the moment she started to question her choices in life. *Had she made the right decisions with the right person? Was there a better choice, an alternate reality with a better life where she would be happy*?

She stayed at the shop a little longer that night, but before she left for home, her dad got her two six-packs of tacos and a pound of fried potato rounds from Taco John's, which was 6 hard or soft tacos and a pound of potato "olays." He knew tacos were one of her favorite foods. When she arrived home, she walked into her house, noticing the flowers from her husband and kids on the kitchen island. The arrangement was so beautiful, with roses and lilies. The lilies smelled so sweet. Lilies were her favorite flower. Stuck in the flowers was a card from her son that said, "I love you, Mommy," and his name was written in his own handwriting. Cheyenne felt loved with how the day went. She hadn't felt that way in a long time. She thought that this had to be the best birthday. Cheyenne felt generally happy, something she hadn't felt in a long time. In fact, she had almost forgotten how being happy felt. She had been out on her mail route for a few hours when she decided to send a text to Sebastian. This was the first time she was going to text him something unrelated to work. She wasn't sure if she should, but finally decided to hit send.

3

"Are you at work?" Cheyenne started.

"Yea. What's up?" Sebastian replied.

"Can I annoy you today?"

"Sure. Are you at the shop?" The reply came within a few seconds.

"No, I am out on my mail route, and I'm getting wet. I hate getting wet." She waited a moment before adding more. "I am wet in places that shouldn't be wet."

"All alone and wet... bummer... Why are you wet, honey?" Sebastian asked.

Cheyenne giggled after reading his response. "Because my window won't roll up, and it is raining. Can you get a window motor for it?" Before he could answer again, she sent, "Yep, no one here but me, all alone and wet."

"Next time take a rubber duck with you and you won't be alone."

"Not my kind of rubber." She rolled her eyes as she answered the message.

"Got to go... Getting busy. I'll talk to you later."

A few hours later when she was at home her phone went off. Cheyenne got up from the chair in the front room to go see who was texting her. It was Sebastian. She was kind of excited to see what he had to say.

"Are you dry yet?" He asked.

"Yes, I am dry. What are you doing?"

"Getting ready to watch the Walking Dead." He replied almost instantly.

"I don't know what that is."

"It's a zombie show."

"Oh, well... I haven't seen it," she said.

"You should watch it; you may like it," he answered. "Got to go... Someone is here."

"Goodnight" she said.

"Goodnight, honey... talk to you tomorrow." He replied.

As the days went by, people around the business started to call her his work wife, all because one day, when she went down the road to the Chrysler dealership, she picked up light bulbs he had ordered for her. The guy called Sebastian afterwards and told him that his wife picked up his parts. So, everyone started to tease the two of them. Cheyenne didn't mind people teasing her about it.

Soon, Cheyenne and Sebastian started texting almost daily. Most of the time their conversations were simple, but it wasn't long before the conversations became personal ... then they became sexual.

One weekend, she decided to get a hotel room to get away for the weekend. She wanted time to hang out with an old friend. They had been friends for years, but they had to stop talking because of the man, Jennie's ex-husband, who came between them. Before Cheyenne had her first-born, she and Jennie were always together. They had a special spot where they would go drink. Jennie's husband at the time got jealous of the bond the two had. Jennie's ex-husband was jealous of Cheyenne. One day Jennie tried to leave him. He accused her of cheating and threated to take her kids from her if she left. Cheyenne supported her friend. Jennie didn't want to lose her kids, so she said she would stay with him. He made her call Cheyenne and tell her that she hated her and never wanted to see here again. He blamed it on Cheyenne, even though Cheyenne lived over an hour away. He forbade Jennie to see or even talk to Cheyenne. He even made her call Cheyenne and tell her that she didn't want to be friends anymore.

When Jennie finally got the courage to leave her ex-husband is when she was finally able to look up Cheyenne. At first, Cheyenne was nervous about being friends again, but soon, they were talking daily, as if nothing ever happened. They vowed that no man would come between them again.

Jennie and Cheyenne bought some alcoholic beverages and headed back to the hotel room. Jennie was shorter than Cheyenne and had reddish-brown hair. She and Cheyenne had matching tattoos of a triquetra on the inside of their right wrist. Jennie's was black, and Cheyenne's tattoo was purple. They got the tattoos when they were in their early 20's. Jennie's personality was like a firecracker small with a short fuse, but it could blow you up at the same time. After they got to the room, they sat around and drank and talked. "We should have gone out to the spot," Cheyenne said.

"Yeah maybe, but it is a little chilly out still." Jennie looked over at Cheyenne, who was staring at her phone. "Just text him, Cheyenne."

"Text who?" Cheyenne asked like she had no idea who Jennie was talking about.

"Text Sebastian. Ask him to hang out with you or give me your phone and I will," Jennie suggested. "Then, if you text him, maybe you will relax a bit."

"Fine. I'll text him. He will probably say no." Cheyenne snorted with a little bit of sass. "She picked up her phone and opened it up to their previous conversation and started a new message.

"So, do you want to hang out with me... when you get off work?" She asked.

"I can't tonight. Got stuff to do. Are you sticking around town tomorrow?" He replied within a few minutes.

"You can't for a few minutes?" She paused for a moment to see if he would reply.

"Yeah, for a while tomorrow. Depends on what time I get out of here. Have to go home and let the dogs out," Sebastian responded. She knew he was hurrying when texting because he almost always used correct grammar in his messages.

"You can do that real fast and then come for one drink with us," she wrote, hoping he would say yes.

"Can I bring Bam Bam?" He asked. She knew he took his dog

everywhere, so the odds of him coming without the dog were slim. Bam Bam was a small dog. He had long black hair and reminded Cheyenne of a shih tzu. She wasn't 100-percent sure what breed he was though. Sebastian didn't go many places without his dog.

"Sure," she responded and sent him a picture of his favorite drinks. Which was Miller Lite and Twisted Tea. She got one of each. She was hoping that it would entice him to come.

"Sweet" was his only reply.

About 15 minutes went by before she received another text message.

"Where are you?" Sebastian asked.

"The hotel." Cheyenne answered.

"Which one?" Sebastian replied.

"Hampton." She felt stupid after she realized that he would need to know which hotel she was staying in.

"Room?" He asked her.

"219" was all she said.

"Here," he replied a few moments later.

"Give me a moment and I will walk down and let you in," she wrote. "He's here. I'll go down and let him in. Do you want to walk down with me?" Cheyenne asked Jennie.

"Naw, I'm good," Jennie replied, not even looking up from her phone. Cheyenne walked down the stairs at a fast pace. She was excited, yet nervous that Sebastian was coming to see her.

He was standing at the entrance with his back to the door. She stopped in front of the door and admired him standing there. Sebastian was older than she was by a little more than 11 years, but she still thought that he was an extremely handsome man. She pushed the door open until it lightly touched him. He turned around and smiled, and the corners of his mouth twitched.

That damn smirk of a smile was what turned her to putty in his hand. His lip pulled up ever so slightly showing a small amount of his teeth, the white glimmering slightly as his gaze met hers. His eyes twinkled slightly with the mirth of knowing that all he had to do was smile and she would be his.

"Jennie is here, too," she informed him as they started up the stairs. He didn't reply, but Cheyenne could tell he didn't look too thrilled that Jennie was there, although she had no idea why. When they got to the room, he sat on the end of the bed, and she sat on the bed across from him. Jennie sat at the top of the bed he was sitting on. They all sat in awkward silence for a moment before Cheyenne broke the silence as she offered him a beer. She couldn't help but think of how handsome he was sitting there. He was still in his black work uniform. He noticed her staring at him. She thought about looking away, but his eyes were locked on hers, and she just couldn't break away from his gaze. He just smiled.

"Thought you were going to bring your dog," Cheyenne said.

"I decided to come here first," Sebastian replied.

"I see," Jennie said.

"So, how do you two know each other?" Cheyenne asked. She had heard bits and pieces of how and she wanted to know both sides of the story.

"We worked together at the old gas station beside your dad's shop," Sebastian explained

"And I know his ex-wife," Jennie answered.

"Who is that?" Cheyenne asked as she glanced back and forth between them.

"Madelyn Hogen," Sebastian answered.

"I don't think I know her," Cheyenne said after a moment of pondering.

Sebastian spoke more than anyone while he was there. He also seemed to fidget. After about an hour of talking, mostly about work, Cheyenne noticed Sebastian seemed to become somewhat uncomfortable.

"I better get going; I still need to let the dogs out," he said as he stood up.

"I'll walk you downstairs," Cheyenne offered as she stood up quickly to follow him out the door. As she was walking out the door, she turned and grinned at Jennie.

As they turned the corner to the stairs Sebastian spoke. "Just so you know, I don't like her at all, and I really don't want to be around her." He paused a moment before reiterating, at all."

The rest of the walk down the stairs was quiet. She didn't really know what to say. Finally, she replied with, "OK." When they arrived at the side door, she stood very close to him for what seemed like an eternity, staring into his eyes. She wanted to kiss him but was unsure if she should blatantly step over the "friend zone." She felt like there was some sort of gravitational pull drawing her to him. This wasn't the first time she had felt this way. She fought back the urge and said, "I'll text you."

"Bye," he replied and walked out the door. She watched him walk to his car, checking out his ass with each step before she walked back up to her room.

As soon as she walked back in the room Jennie started probing her. "So, did you kiss him?"

"No, I did not kiss him," she said as she flopped down on the bed. She laid there staring at the ceiling for a moment. "But I wanted too so badly. He smelled so good," she added as she sat up. "Ugh, I'm pretty sure he doesn't like me like that anyway."

"You don't know that. You should ask him," Jennie replied, pouring them another shot of Crown. "Just text him and ask him if he wanted you to kiss him. Or, give me your phone and I will text him for you."

"I don't know if I can ask him that." She paused and looked at her phone. "What can it hurt? I mean, he could just say he doesn't like me that way."

"Right. I doubt he'll say that, but just ask." She handed Cheyenne the shot glass. "Take the shot, Cheyenne. Maybe it will give you the courage to ask what you want to ask."

Cheyenne stared at the shot glass for a moment and gave it a couple swirls before shooting it down. She and Jennie talked about what they should do. Cheyenne suggested, "Let's go for a drive."

"Jennie is laughing at me; she thinks I should've kissed you. What do you think?" Cheyenne wrote in a text to Sebastian. "Oh, and by the way, I'm pretty sure you owe me pictures." Sebastian promised her a naughty picture of him because she sent him one, but he kept chickening out on her. Cheyenne was beginning to think that he was never going to follow through.

"We will talk about it tomorrow," he responded. There were a few moments between texts. "Both actually."

Cheyenne waited a moment before replying. "Just tell me in a text. I can handle it." She wasn't sure how long of a pause there was between their responses. He didn't even have to text her; she knew what he was going to say to her, about both subjects.

"Look, I like you, but there is too much to be lost." he finally confessed. She was right. She felt like she was hit with a ton of bricks straight in her forehead.

"It's all right. It's just fun and games. Harmless texting." It was the only reply she could muster. The figurative bricks that struck her began the onset of a series of headaches, as though it were a literal blow to the head.

4

It had been a month since that night they had hung out. The conversations between the two of them had become more intense. Cheyenne would text him every morning, telling him "Good morning." Sebastian would end their conversation every night with a "Goodnight." They talked almost every night on her way home from work. Cheyenne looked forward to his messages. When he couldn't message her, she felt sad. She would be left wondering if she had done something wrong. She would start to question herself. Was she rude? Maybe she made him mad. Cheyenne struggled with the filter on her mouth and could often speak more bluntly on a topic than she intended. But then the next morning he would reply to her good morning text." He made her heart melt.

The day was April 17, the day that she knew she could never go back to the way her life was before. She pulled into town, and seeing that he was at work, she decided to go in and see him. When she walked through the double doors, she was greeted by his seductive smile.

"Hey, Honey, what are you doing here?" Sebastian asked.

"I'm in town for the weekend. I wanted to see if you would like to hang out. He was standing beside the counter. She could see he was wearing his black work pants with a red screwdriver slightly sticking out of his left front hip pocket. His knife was hooked on his right hip pocket, and his black shirt, on which his name was sewn, had two pens in the front pocket. She couldn't believe how handsome he looked in his work attire.

"You look nice," he said. She was wearing a light-purple shirt with a slender gray sweater wrapped around her arms, and she sported a pair of holey jeans. She noticed Sebastian looking her up and down, which made her feel good.

"Thank you," she said with a smile. "So do you want to hang out?"

"Sure, it will have to be later this evening. Will you pick me up something to drink?" He asked.

"Yeah, I can. I'll text you where I'm staying."

"Ok," he said as he waved goodbye.

Cheyenne went back to the hotel. The one she chose this time was a smoking room. She didn't smoke, but she knew that Sebastian would stay longer if he didn't have to go outside to smoke. The room had two beds and looked a little rough. You could tell that it had not been fully redone after the last horrible storm the town had endured. The carpet was an orange color. There was a small fridge in the corner of the room by the window, out of which she could see the gas station across the road.

She sat on the edge of the bed, nervous, afraid that he wouldn't show up. She decided to take a shot of Peach Crown while she waited for him. The phone started playing the song, "Lips of an Angel." She knew that was his text tone. She got up and grabbed the phone off the table.

"What room are you in?" Sebastian wrote.

"215" was her reply. She started to get really nervous. She was beginning to really like him. She thought about all the fun that they had when they were together or even when they were just talking on the phone.

~~~~

Cheyenne checked her appearance in the mirror before she headed to the door. Her blonde, curly hair hung to her shoulders. She wished she would have put on some sort of make-up besides the eyeliner. She was glad that the eyeliner made her green eyes look more like a brochure advertising for the waters of the Caribbean Islands. She unlocked the door to the hotel room. He was dressed in casual attire, a faded-green hoodie with worn-out, light-blue jeans. The tightness of his jeans made his ass look firm as he walked through the door and towards the bed.

He sat on the edge of the bed, the corner that overlooked the city below. She followed behind him and sat on the same side of the bed but more towards the headboard.
~~~~

Resting one foot behind him, slightly touching him with it, she let the other foot dangle off the bed and nervously painted shapes and letters with her toe. She could tell that he was nervous to be there alone with her. He made it clear to her that he just wanted to hang out. That's it. There was so much that she wanted to say or do to him in her mind.

"Would you like a drink?" Cheyenne asked. "I got some beer."

"Yes, that would be good." Sebastian paused a moment and then took a drink of the Miller Light she had handed him. "Sarah doesn't know that I am here. No phones or pictures on Facebook, please."

"I won't say anything to her, Sebastian. No one will know."

"Have you listened to the songs that I suggested to you by Blue October?" He asked her.

"Yeah, there are a few I like." They both sat there listening to music and talking about songs they both liked, contemplating bad decisions they could be making...or were about to make? She didn't realize that some of the songs he selected were chosen specifically for her.

"Cheyenne, I really must be going."

"Yes," she stood up, pretending to allow him to leave without any form of a fight. Upon standing, she became light-headed and stumbled into his arms. He must have been unprepared to catch her because they both fell onto the bed. As she stared into his blue eyes, the next thing she knew he was kissing her...and she was kissing him back. His kisses were rough but not unwanted, and the passion began to build. He slid his hand up her shirt as if to see if her breasts matched the image he had concocted in his head. Suddenly he went on sensory overload and pushed away from her.

"We cannot be doing this. Really, we cannot do this at all," Sebastian said as he stood to his feet, sounding as if he really meant it this time. For a brief moment, he turned his body around to face the window and then turned back towards her. She was unaware of what was going through his mind.

"I am fully aware that we shouldn't be doing this," she said as she reached for his hands. He took her hands and pulled her up to him, trying to ward off any chance of her moving things forward. She kept changing the rules of this game, as she slid a hand up the back of his shirt. She put her lips to his. Like a train careening off a track, he practically conceded in a loss, and then, in a victorious manner, he quickly pulled her light-purple shirt up over her head, his eyes never leaving hers. Then he pulled his shirt over his head. Cheyenne was lost in his eyes. She felt as if he were peering into her soul.

He slid his hand lightly down her shoulders, and the touch of his hands sent shivers up her spine. She has never done anything like this before...well, she has, but only inside her own imagination. But this was real. *Wait, this is real*! She had never felt the way he made her feel. His hands made their way to her breasts. He bent down and lightly touched her nipples with his tongue. Her nipples were even more beautiful than he had imagined. Now they were erect and so was he. A moan escaped her lips, as his tongue licked and twirled around her nipples. He brought his lips back up to hers, thrusting his tongue into her mouth, exploring it with every kiss. She wrapped her arms around him.

They both collapsed back onto the bed as he kissed everywhere on her chest, making sure that no part was neglected. Sebastian stood again. This time leaving was no longer an option as he began unbuttoning her pants. He slowly lifted her legs and slid her pants off; the only resistance were the fibers in her jeans. She now laid there in nothing but her purple lace bra and underwear. Her bra was halfway pushed up, revealing both of her breasts. He lightly tugged at her underwear. She thought for a moment that he was going to rip them off her, but instead, he slowly and steadily pulled them down and slipped them off, seeming to drink in the moment as if it were a fine wine to be savored. He stood above her wearing only his jeans. Clearly, he was overdressed for this occasion. She attempted to reach up to undo his belt when he pushed her back onto the bed. It became a battle of control, but Cheyenne began to plead with him, almost begging for his throbbing cock. "I need you!" She knew she was practically begging him, showing him that she was devoid of any poker face, and with a sleight of hand, he continued to drive her absolutely crazy.

Dropping to his knees, he let out a low, guttural growl and ran his hands down her thighs. He suddenly wrapped his arms around her legs and pulled her to the side of the bed, almost declaring some form of ownership in a primitive way. The conquest was just beginning...he started just above her knee. Sebastian began kissing her inner thighs and slowly dragging his lips down one inner thigh and up the inside of the other. As he kissed her thighs, he ran his hands up and down her legs. She could feel her ability to retain control (or *lack thereof*) slipping away from her as his tongue began to slip inside of her lips. She didn't know what to do. In ways she wanted him to stop, but in ways she never wanted him to stop. She was unsure how long she was going to be able to keep from cumming when he had barely even touched her.

She couldn't hold back the moans, so she stopped trying to repress them. He slowly nibbled on her clitoris. She wasn't completely sure what he was doing to her down there, but if she were a vault, he was cracking her code to get into her black box. With each lick, he was swiping left, swiping right, and waiting to see if he had her full approval. She whipped her head right toward him and he knew that he was the puppet master, pulling at every string. He played her like a guitar in need of tuning. Her moans became delicate cries, and she became hoarse from exerting her vocal cords so intensely. Even he could not stop. He just kept lapping at her, playing her body like a fine-tuned instrument. Her body rose off the bed, and she arched her back, thinking about how much control she was relinquishing. "Oh, my God! Please, Sebastian, I need you" pretty much sealed her fate as she made her needs known out loud. She ran her fingers over the top of his head and gave a small tug on his hair. "Come here," she said with a slight quiver in her voice.

Sebastian looked up and into the luminous, beautiful green of her eyes. "Cheyenne, we can do a lot, but I cannot be inside you. All right?"

"Yes, I understand," she said as he continued kissing her all over. She felt as if he may be losing control of what he wanted to do to her. He slid a finger inside of her, rubbing her interior and then sliding it between the lips, and then inside again, which made her gasp and then subsequently shiver He continued that series of motions repeatedly. When she was really moving to the rhythm of his hands, Sebastian just stopped.

He confidently came up to settle himself on top of her, but he was lightly holding himself up, just above her. They both knew that he had the upper hand. "What do you really want?" He playfully asked, although just hearing it out loud is what he wanted more than anything. Well, hearing that and having his dick inside her. She could taste herself on his lips and he thought she was sweet and succulent like a juicy piece of meat, but one that he could devour with all his senses and keep coming back for more.

She bit her lower lip and contemplated for a moment. "You know what I want? I want you inside of me." He stood up. She thought he was going to walk away, however, instead, it was as though he were a stoic gladiator, but the look in his eyes showed he couldn't, wouldn't back down. This time he wasn't even attempting to leave. He was now going to accommodate her, and while reaching for the button of his jeans, she beat him to it. The button was hot. It didn't matter why it was hot; neither of them was about to heed this warning, if that is what this was. What mattered was the fact that the jeans needed to be shed like a snake that sheds its skin for new life.

Sebastian was going to pump new life into Cheyenne's body, and she was ready for it. In fact, they were both ready. While kissing his cheek, a sensual, gravitational pull descended over her. She began to hit sensory overload. She let her desires overcome her, as she explored his neck, working her way down...and further down... Using her tongue, she continued tasting his skin. She teased him with her feminine charms, using her tongue to explore his upper body as she ran her finger over his nipples. She gripped his ass with one arm and used her free hand to unhook his belt. She struggled to unhook his pants with one hand, so she pulled her other arm from behind him and successfully unbuttoned his fly.

She was having trouble concentrating on what she was doing while he was kissing her neck and sliding a finger inside of her. "Mmmm, ahhh" she moaned.

Finally, his pants dropped around his ankles. He lightly stepped out of them and stood there in his boxers. She reached over and gripped his hard cock though his underwear. Just touching him turned her on even more. She felt like an oven, hot to the touch. They locked eyes as she rubbed him. Slowly, he reached down and grabbed her wrist with one hand to stop her. He raised her hand to his chest, then he grabbed his boxers in each hand and pulled them off his waist, allowing them to drop to the floor.

He pushed her down on the bed and climbed on top of her, pinning her hands slightly above her head. He started by kissing her neck, as he slowly slid inside her. She thought he was going to be gentle, but his thrusts were fast and hard. It wasn't long before he finished. He collapsed on top of her before he began the mumbling all over again. “This was such a mistake, and this shouldn't be happening..." he continued. She wasn't sure if the tears he displayed were from the thought of giving into his desires. When she enticed him further, he edged his way diagonally off the bed. She slightly covered his lips with her index finger as if she could silence his conscience with such the slightest touch. How naive of her... how naive of him. With one finger attempting to shush his mumbles, she moved forward to conjure up her powers of persuasion and began to kiss down his neck, making her way down to his aching cock.

She slightly slid the tip of his cock in her mouth, twirling her tongue around the slit, and with every groan, she swirled her tongue more, until she finally thrusted his cock deep into her mouth. She sucked and teased and played all at the same time. She gripped his balls with one hand and rubbed them as she moved his cock in and out of her mouth. She loved nibbling on the tip. He would moan, and the more he moaned, the more it turned her on, and the harder she sucked. Sebastian started to move his hips with her rhythm.

He took her by surprise when he pulled her onto his face, but she continued to suck his cock profusely. The pleasure he started to give her was so intense that she could no longer concentrate on what she was doing to him. If this was a game, she wanted to make sure that she would be coming out on top. She decided to swing around, facing him. He watched her climb on top of him and then he watched as she slipped his engorged, throbbing cock into her. He grabbed her hands with his and used her hands to pin his own hands down. She felt as if she were in control, yet she knew this act of submission by him was only an act. She was completely turned on by the force he was using to hold her hands to his and to the bed. She gave up trying to take her hands away from his and just accepted she was no longer in control. As soon as she submitted to his control, they moved together in synchronous rhythm. Within a few movements of her hips, she collapsed on top of him, struggling to catch her breath. He wrapped his arms around her, kissing her intensely as he continued to move his hips. Even with her on top of him, he was still able to slam himself inside of her, until he felt himself explode inside her walls.

5

She laid on top of him for a moment, just looking into his eyes, and they kissed a few more times. He smiled his special smile and it started to turn her on again. "Wow!" was the only response she could muster, as he was running his fingers up and down her arms. "That was amazing!" Cheyenne said.

"That it was." He paused for a moment. "What time is it? I have to get back to the house before she gets off work."

"It is almost 8 o'clock." Cheyenne replied.

"I really need to get going, but I need to take a shower before I go," he said as he slightly lifted her off him.

"Why do you have to shower? Do you really have to go?" She asked in a pleading voice.

"Yes, I have to go. I can't go home smelling like another woman." He stood up and pulled her up beside him. He gave her a quick kiss and headed towards the shower. She followed behind him. He turned on the shower faucet and climbed in. She stepped in behind him and ran her hands down his back and slowly around to his front. She kissed his back. "I really have to go," he insisted as he turned around to face her.

"All right," she said with a pouty face. She tried to give him the biggest lip quiver she could muster, hoping that her expression would make him want to stay longer. All it did was make him smile at her.

"I can see you tomorrow after she goes to work," he said as he kissed her forehead.

"I don't think I will be able to see you. My son's party is tomorrow."

"Then we can text, and you can call me when you have time," Sebastian said as he stepped out of the shower. He grabbed his towel and headed to find his clothes. She grabbed a towel, too, and followed him out of the bathroom. As she started getting dressed, he asked, "Are you going to walk me down?"

"Yeah, I can," she responded, pulling up her pants. As she was pulling her shirt over her head her phone started to ring. She looked over at the bedside table to see who was calling. She saw it was Jennie and hit ignore.

"Who was that?" Sebastian asked. "You do know you can answer it, right?"

"Yeah, it was Jennie. I'll call her back. She just wants to know what I am doing. I was supposed to meet her at the casino." She paused for a moment. "Like an hour ago," she said with a small chuckle.

They both finished dressing and headed out of the room, and by the time they hit the stairs, her phone rang again. It was Jennie again. She looked at him before she answered. "Yes, I'm heading to the casino now."

"Don't worry about it, we'll meet you at Applebee's," Jennie said.

"Here in town?"

"Duh! Yes, here in town." Jennie replied.

"Ok, I'll head there now." She hung up the phone and continued walking down the stairs.

They stood at the door for a moment before walking out. "I'll talk to you later," Sebastian said as he opened the door. She wanted to pull him into a kiss, but he must have read her mind because he gently pulled her to him and embraced her in a hug. He gave her a small peck on the forehead before he turned and walked outside to their cars.

Before they could get into their vehicles, Cheyenne's phone was ringing. They both looked down at it at the same time. "You better get that. We will talk tomorrow," Sebastian assured her as he opened his car door.

"Ok," She answered as she got into her Jeep. "Bye," she said shutting her door and starting her Jeep.

~~~~

She followed him out of the parking lot and down Main Street. She turned left and pulled into Applebee's, and he kept going straight. Jennie
~~~~

was waiting by the entrance to the restaurant but walked over to the Jeep when she saw Cheyenne pull into the parking lot. As she was pulling in, she received a new text message. It was from her dad. "While some people are out whoring around, other people are being family people, taking care of kids... yuuuuuup have fun...don't drink and drive."

She smiled; her dad was being his normal annoying self. "I'm not even drinking, and if I do, I'll call and have you come get me," she responded."

"Ok gulping," he wrote.

"What is gulping?" Cheyenne asked her dad, even though she was pretty sure she didn't want to know the answer. When he didn't reply, she shoved the phone into the pocket of her hoodie.

Jennie barely waited for the vehicle to come to a stop in the parking space. "Dean and I have been waiting for you. What have you been doing? Where have you been? Your hair is a mess." Jennie said with a big grin.

"I fell asleep," Cheyenne replied hoping that it was dark enough and Jennie couldn't see her facial expressions.

"Sure, you did." Jennie replied with a hint of sarcasm in her voice.

"Really, I did," Cheyenne said with a grin on her face. Jennie knew that she was bluffing her, but she let it go since Dean was right there.

It wasn't long after Cheyenne got to Applebee's that the pager went off, letting them know there was a table ready.

"Let's go get some food, ladies," Dean said as he started toward the restaurant. Jennie and Cheyenne proceeded to get out of her Jeep and follow Dean, who held the door open for them. He was about the same height as Cheyenne, and he had sandy-blond hair. He was a nicely built man with beautiful blue eyes.

As they walked into the restaurant, Jennie looked over at Cheyenne and giggled.

"What are you laughing at, Jennie?"

"Nothing," she replied with another small chuckle.

Cheyenne rolled her eyes at Jennie. She knew her friend knew something was up. She wanted to tell her what just happened, but she didn't want Dean to know. They went inside and followed the waitress to a booth at the back of the restaurant. Cheyenne sat down and Jennie slipped in next to her. Dean sat across from them. Cheyenne opened her phone to see another message from her dad. “Chugging and getting laid. Shhhhhhh, secret safe with me...... No more kids.”

“Ok, who do you think I'm with?” She asked him.

“Pull out now, talk tomorrow.... Yuuup!” He responded.

“Jennie, look at these messages from my dad.” She showed her what he sent.

“Let's send him a picture of us together,” Jennie said, and they snapped a group picture and sent it to him.

It didn’t take long for her dad to send a message back. “Oh, fuck, it’s getting perverted. Don’t want any details. I’ll take care of your child. Mum’s the word...yuuuuup.” They both giggled at his reply.

The waitress stood in front of the booth. “Can I start you guys out with some drinks?” They each ordered a mixed drink. Cheyenne was pretty sure the couple shots of Peach Crown she took before Sebastian came out to the hotel room were more than enough to drink, but she ordered a mixed drink anyway. Cheyenne ordered steak and shrimp with mashed potatoes and broccoli. Jennie and Dean each ordered a steak. There was a lot of small talk over dinner, however, it was Dean and Jennie who did most of the talking.

Cheyenne really had nothing much to say; she was lost in her thoughts from her pre-dinner romp with Sebastian. She could not believe the incredible night she had, had so far.

“Jennie, can you let me out? I need to go to the bathroom,” she asked as she started to stand up.

“Yeah, I have to go, too.” Cheyenne knew she was just going so they could be alone, so she could ask questions.

They walked down the hall to the restroom, and neither of them spoke a word. As soon as they stepped into the restroom, Jennie spoke. “Spill!” Cheyenne ignored her and walked into the stall. “Come on, Cheyenne! I know something happened."

“Nothing happened. The only thing we did was sit and listen to music and talk. We kissed a little, and that is all.”

"Well, why not more?" Jennie asked as Cheyenne walked out of the stall to wash her hands.

"Because nothing happened. Maybe he doesn't like me in that way." Cheyenne did not like lying to her friend, but she wasn't sure if Sebastian would want anyone to know. While Jennie was washing her hands, Cheyenne took out her phone. She was hoping Sebastian had messaged her. After a quick glance, she saw that he had not. She was slightly disappointed that she didn't get any messages from him, even though she knew he wouldn't message because of the time. She knew his girlfriend was likely at home. They walked back to the table to see that Dean was done eating and ready to go.

"Are you guys going home?" Cheyenne asked as they walked out to their cars.

"Yeah, probably," Jennie replied. "Why?"

"No reason. I guess I'm going to head back to the hotel then. What time are you off work tomorrow?"

"I get off at 3," Jennie said. "Will you still be in town?"

"Yeah. Dad and I are going to work on some cars. Then we are going to his house for supper. Well, it will be the kids and me."

"I'll just call you when I get off work to see what you are doing."

"All right. Thank you for dinner, Dean," Cheyenne said as she stopped at her Jeep, her hand on the door handle.

"You're welcome," Dean said. They all said their goodbyes and got in their cars. Cheyenne drove her car back to the hotel. When she arrived, she just sat there in her Jeep. She couldn't stop thinking about what had happened earlier. She broke into a big grin and then let out a little sigh. She kept wishing she would be going back to the room to him, but she knew she was just being wishful.

Sebastian had made her feel so important. She had not felt like that in a long time. She walked up to the room and sat on the edge of the bed, the same place where he sat a few hours earlier. She ran her fingers over the sheets and then got up and grabbed a pair of shorts and a top from her bag and slipped them on. She laid down in the bed and took in a huge breath. She could smell his sweet scent on the pillow next to her.

Cheyenne figured she had better try to get some sleep, so she rolled over, grabbed her phone, and turned her playlist on low. She was pretty sure she would not sleep much but closed her eyes anyway. She drifted off to the sound of *'Need you now'* by Lady A. Her mind landed on Sebastian as the words of the song rang through her head: *Reaching for the phone 'cause I can't fight it anymore, and I wonder if I ever cross your mind.* The next thing she knew her alarm was going off and it was morning. When Cheyenne woke up the next morning, she was unsure whether last had night really happened. It felt like it was all just a dream. She picked up her phone to text Sebastian, then she remembered that she couldn't text him until after 2 p.m. She got up to shower and got dressed to go help her dad since there was work to be done at the shop. She really wasn't in the mood to work on anything. She just really wanted to talk to Sebastian.

6

Upon arrival at the shop, she realized that her dad wasn't even there yet. While she waited for him, she decided to clean up the office and work on paperwork. Once he showed up, they started to work on cars and get a few things done. She remembered she needed to text her husband, Alan, and tell him what time to bring the kids over. She grabbed her phone and sent a quick text. "Hey, bring Behrad over to Dad's about 4. At least leave the house by 4." Behrad was her 4-year-old son. She knew that she wouldn't get a response from her husband. She rarely got any answers from him. To her surprise, he sent a message back. "Ok. We will leave at 4. Do we need to bring anything?"

"No, I don't think so," she responded. Then, she went off to do more of the paperwork.

She decided to send a text to Sebastian. "He's at the shop if you still want to come down and tighten your lug nuts." She didn't get a reply, so she went back to sorting the paperwork. She wasn't supposed to text him before 2 p.m. unless it was work related. The door to the shop opened and then quickly closed. She looked up to see Sabrina walking in.

"Hey, Sabrina. What are you doing here?" Cheyenne asked.

"I have to go get one of the kids from their mom's and we don't really get along, which makes me not want to go alone. I was going to ask if you would take me to get her?" Sabrina was about as tall as Cheyenne. She had a haircut that reminded her of a bob, short hair on the bottom and longer hair on top. She always wore her hair on top of her head in a short ponytail. Right now, her hair was a greenish-blue color. Sabrina was not a big woman by any means, but she was not a small woman either. She always wore long men's shorts and laced-up boots.

"Sure, I can run you over. Where do we have to pick her up?" Cheyenne asked. She didn't really want to go anywhere since Sebastian might come down to the shop. She wanted to see him. She felt like she needed to see him.

"I have to get her from Gilman. I have to have her picked up by 2," Sabrina said. Cheyenne looked down at her phone to see what time it was. It was 1:15. Before she could say anything else, Sebastian pulled up to the shop door. She went to open her mouth to say something to Sabrina, but nothing came out.

He walked into the office wearing a black T-shirt and light-blue pants. The pants appeared to be the same ones from the night before. "Where is your daddy?" He looked Cheyenne up and down and then broke into a big grin, which made Cheyenne grin. She felt sexy in her silver jeans and her cute pink tank top. She always felt cute when he looked at her and smiled. She thought he had a special smile that he revealed only to her.

"He's in the shop, as far as I know," Cheyenne replied. Sebastian walked over to her and handed her his dog, Bam. He turned on his heels and headed to the back area to the shop. "Yeah, Sabrina, I can take you, Cheyenne said, putting away her papers. "Let's head out to the Jeep."

"Are we taking Bam?" Sabrina asked as she looked down at the dog in Cheyenne's arms.

"No. He'll come get him as soon as I start my Jeep. He will come running out. He will definitely get mad at me if I steal his dog," she said as she headed out the front door. She wasn't wrong. As soon as she started her Jeep, he came out of the huge overhead garage door to get his dog. Bam crawled up her arms, away from Sebastian. Cheyenne giggled and handed his dog back to him.

"Are you leaving?" He asked her as he cocked an eyebrow at her.

"Yeah, we have to run to Gilman. She has to pick up her stepdaughter. We will be back in a bit. How long will you be here?"

"Not very long. Just going to tighten my lug nuts. Then I have to head home. I have a few things I need to get done around the house today."

"Oh, well I'll text you then." Cheyenne replied. Sabrina and Cheyenne got in the Jeep. Cheyenne started to back out of the parking place beside Sebastian's car. He smiled again and waved at her, moving only his fingers. Both women looked at each other and started to giggle.

They drove to Gilman mostly in silence before Sabrina spoke up. "Spill the beans, now."

"Spill what? There's nothing to say," Cheyenne said as she broke into a half smirk.

"Liar. I know something happened last night. I was just in the same place as you both. Obviously, something happened. Sebastian looked at you as if you had no clothes on at all." Sabrina paused for a moment. "So, spill it. How did last night go? I know you two were going to hang out."

"Well..." Cheyenne started to say when Sabrina interrupted her.

"You guys did it, didn't you?"

It was a few awkward moments before Cheyenne could muster a reply. She could feel her ears turning red. She wanted to tell her friend, but she also didn't want to make Sebastian angry. "You cannot say a word to anyone. Promise me!"

Sabrina broke into a huge smile. "Of course. I won't say a word to anyone. Come on, tell me what happened."

"Yes, we had sex. It was amazing. He was all about me. Like, I have never had sex like that before. I don't know how to explain it to you." As Cheyenne rambled, she could feel her face burning as the memory of last night flooded her mind. Cheyenne filled her in on the details, even the strange texts from her dad.

"Yay! I'm happy for you. I am going to be honest with you, it's about time." Sabrina hooted.

"Why is it 'about time?'" Cheyenne asked. She really had no idea why Sabrina would make such a declaration.

"Because there is so much sexual tension between you two. Everyone can see it. Well, except the two of you."

"Ummm, I don't know about that," Cheyenne said.

"It is true. You ask Jennie or anyone at his work and they will tell you the same thing."

"OK." Cheyenne did not want to ask anyone about that subject. She knew Sebastian didn't like Jennie, and he definitely didn't want anyone from his work to know what happened.

They arrived at the house where they had to pick up Sabrina's step-daughter. While Sabrina was inside the house, she decided to send a text to Sebastian.

"Are you still at the shop?" Cheyenne asked.

It wasn't long before he replied. "Nope."

"What time do you work tomorrow? I have a surprise."

It was a few minutes before he replied to her. "7, I think."

"Hmm, well could you check?" Cheyenne asked.

"I am going in at 7," he replied.

Sabrina wasn't in the house very long before she came back outside. The ride back to town was quiet. Neither said anything, but Sabrina kept looking over at Cheyenne and smiling at her.

"You know you're creeping me out. Stop staring at me," Cheyenne said.

"Pshh. Does he know that you were going to tell me?" Sabrina asked, cocking her head slightly to the side and lifting an eyebrow.

"No, he doesn't know. And you CANNOT tell him. He would be pissed at me."

"Calm down, Cheyenne. I won't say anything. I promise." Sabrina leaned closer to Cheyenne and said in a near whisper, "Was it at least worth it?"

"Yes, it most definitely was. He was amazing. I really hope that there is a next time," Cheyenne said with a huge grin on her face. She could feel her cheeks turning red again. "You can't say anything to Dad either," she said as she pulled into the shop.

"I won't, don't worry. Your secret is safe with me," Sabrina said as she opened the door to the Jeep and jumped out.

~~~~

Cheyenne's dad was standing by the overhead door. "Are you ready to go to Hy-Vee? I believe we have a cake to get little man for his birthday," he said. "Sabrina, are you coming with us?"
~~~~

"Sure, we can come." They all piled back into the Jeep. This time Sabrina and her stepdaughter were in the back seat. Cheyenne's dad drove, and Cheyenne was sitting in the front seat. No one said a word the whole ride across town. When they arrived at Hy-Vee, they all headed towards the bakery department.

"I'm going to find some whipped cream," Sabrina said.

"Gee, wonder what you're using that for?" Cheyenne's dad answered.

"Umm, pie...." Sabrina stuttered.

"Sure, it's going to be used for pie," he returned.

Sabrina didn't say anything, but her face was bright red. Cheyenne just rolled her eyes. She knew that her dad was just trying to get Sabrina going.

"Cheyenne!" She heard her dad say in a loud voice. She turned to see him standing by a table of cucumbers. He had a large one in his hand. "You can use this one... and when you're done, you can eat it." Cheyenne's face turned dark red. Cheyenne grew up down the road from Sabrina. She was younger. They had been friends since Cheyenne was in junior high.

"Dad, you can eat the real thing, too, when you're done with it." She couldn't believe that she was having this type of conversation with her dad in the store. Her dad just shook his head at her reply and dropped the cucumber on the table.

"Really, kid. Get your mind out of the gutter," he said.

"Oh yeah, it's me who needs to get my mind out of the gutter, huh? I'm pretty sure you started it," Cheyenne said. Some days her dad annoyed the crap out of her. She did love that he joked with her all the time.

"Nope. It wasn't me," he claimed. Sabrina came walking up and Cheyenne's dad teased her mercilessly. "Did you get your cream?" He asked before breaking into a chuckle.

"Yes, I did," she replied as her face turned red again. "And it is for my pie," Sabrina added.

"I'm ready to go, Dad. I got the cake I want." She chose a white cake with white frosting, upon which she had the cake decorators place a scene of Mickey and Minnie Mouse on the beach and inscribe it with "Happy Birthday, Behrad" in red.

"Well, let's go check out," her dad said. They all checked out and headed back to the shop, where everyone said their goodbyes. Cheyenne and her dad rode to the house together. He didn't have his truck at the shop because he had brought his tractor into town to be worked on so he could sell it.

7

The ride back to her parents' house was quiet. She didn't feel like talking. Besides, her mind was all over the place. Once back at her dad's house, her dad asked if she would take his dog for a walk to calm her down before all the kids got there. She grabbed the leash and his dog and headed out for a walk. During the walk she decided to text Sebastian. "Tell me when you are leaving for work tomorrow so I can send you a video... unless you want me to send it now. You can call me if you want."

"Go ahead and send it," he quickly responded.

"Ok. Well, since I was a wee bit shy and little bit flustered..." she replied.

"Shy... You were being shy?"

"Yes... Couldn't you tell?" She waited a moment before she sent another message. "Nothing?"

"Trying to get some stuff done around the house, Dear. And you were anything but shy."

Cheyenne smiled. She loved talking to him. It made her feel happy. When she was with him, she felt safe. She thought for a moment before answering him. "That doesn't sound like fun. And I am shy. I don't have a lot of experience."

"You could have fooled me."

"Why do you think that? Yeah soooo..."

"That was not shy... Just saying," his text said.

"Well...difference of opinion. LOL. I'm sticking to my story." She giggled as she hit send and then quickly started another message. "I have a question... Have you ever done this before?"

"Which part?" He asked.

"The cheating part... well obviously I have had sex before." She added a kissy emoji at the end of that last line. "I have never cheated on my husband before," she added.

"Neither have I."

"I figured. But... Umm I enjoyed every minute of it. If that helps."

His answer made her blush. "Me, too."

"Honestly, did you think it would happen?" She asked him.

"No, I didn't think I would let myself."

"Yeah well... didn't work so good. My apologies." She waited for a response and when she didn't get one, she sent another message. "What are you doing?"

"Yeah....... I bet you're really sorry."

"Don't believe me? I'm an innocent angel. The bigger question.... Did you want to?" She asked him.

"Yes... but you know it can't keep happening."

"Yes, I'm aware, but if we are speaking the truth, I would like it to. However, I do understand why it can't."

"Me, too, but there is too much to be lost."

"Can I ask you a personal question?" Cheyenne wrote. She was afraid that he would say no.

"Sure," he responded.

"Are you truly happy? I can explain if you need me to," she added.

"Explain."

"Are you happy in your relationship, in your life? Is this how you wanted your life to be forever? I'm not asking this because of yesterday. I have been wanting to ask you for a while, but I didn't want to fuck up our friendship." If she was being honest with herself, he made her nervous. No man had ever made her apprehensive about speaking her mind.

A few minutes elapsed before he sent a message back. "There are other places that I would rather live and other jobs I would rather do, but I'm getting too old to start over again."

"That doesn't really answer the question, and you're not that old, silly."

"Sure, it does."

"Sebastian, not really. That doesn't tell me if you're happy. Besides, you are good at your job and people respect you, and from what I hear, some of the customers don't like talking to other employees."

"I am happy enough." That was the extent of his response.

She figured he would be quiet for a while. She knew he didn't like talking about his feelings. So, she just dropped it for now. She walked the dog back to her dad's house.

It wasn't long before Alan brought her son to her. His 4th birthday party was simple. He was excited about his gifts and his cake and ran around the yard, playing with her sister's kids until the sun went down and they were ready to head home.

Cheyenne was saying her goodbyes when she got a message. She unlocked her phone to see who it was. "Let me know when you leave..."

"Ok. We are saying our goodbyes," she responded to Sebastian. It was about 10 minutes before she texted him again. "We are leaving."

"Call you in a bit. Trying not to get electrocuted," was his next reply.

"Ok," she said. It was about another 15 to 20 minutes before her phone started to ring. It startled her; she had picked a different ringtone for him that day. It was the song 'Addicted To' by Saving Abel. She caught herself singing a few words of the song before she answered his call.

"Hello," she answered.

"Hey, Babe." His voice rang through the phone. "How is your drive?"

"It is all right. Everyone already fell asleep. What are you doing?"

"Just sitting down. Getting ready to head to bed. How was your day?" He asked her, letting out a yawn. She could tell he was tired by the sound of his voice.

"It was pretty good. How was yours?" She asked him. "Sebastian? I have a question. Can I tell either Jennie or Sabrina?"

"My day was pretty good." He paused for a long moment. She thought he had hung up was just about to say something when he spoke again. “I would rather you tell Sabrina. I don’t really care for Jennie, and I don’t trust her not to tell.”

“Ok, I won't tell Jennie. I trust her and I know she wouldn’t say anything to anyone. I wish you both would give each other another chance.”

“Maybe someday. Honey, I have to cut this short. She will be home soon, and I still need to eat supper. Talk to you in the morning?” He asked.

“Yeah, are you mad at me?”

“No, Honey, I'm not mad. I just have things to do before I go to bed.”

She really didn’t want to get off the phone with him. “Ok. I’ll text you in the morning. Goodnight.”

“Text me in the morning. You can stop and see me on the way to the shop.” He paused. “Besides, I think I have parts tickets for you anyway.” Sebastian paused a moment before he spoke again. “Goodnight, Honey,” he said before hanging up the phone. Cheyenne hated the evenings because she couldn’t talk to him anymore.

She decided to call Sabrina. The phone rang a few times before she picked up. “Hey,” she answered.

“Hey, I'm driving home from dad's house. I just got off the phone with Sebastian.”

“And what did he have to say?” She asked.

“He told me I could tell you but not Jennie. Little does he know that I already told you.” Cheyenne giggled. “Oh, my God, I really hope that happens again. It was amazing! He is so yummy. He is so lick-able.”

“We need a name for him because when we text, I'm tired of texting work husband and husband. We could use the emoji that is a lollipop. Because you are always telling me that he is so ‘lick-able’. What do you think?”

“Lollipop, huh. Yeah, we could. You'll have to send me the emoji that you are talking about. I don't know if I have ever seen one, but you use emojis more than I do,” Cheyenne said. “I hate the evening.”

“Why do you hate the evening?”

“Because I don’t get to talk to him anymore. He stops talking to me around 9 and it sucks. I feel so lonely when I can’t talk to him.”

"I know how you feel. I'm home alone at night. Louis works nights, so he doesn't get off work until midnight. I cannot really text him because he is at work. So, I get it."

"How do you make it through the night?" Cheyenne asked.

"It is hard, but you will get used to it. You know what I think?" Sabrina asked.

"What do you think? I am going to go crazy?" She asked sarcastically.

"No, I think that you are falling for him, and if you aren't careful, you are going to get hurt."

"I'm not falling for him. I just like him. I will be fine. We are just friends. I enjoy his friendship, and I definitely think he is yummy. I like other parts of him, too."

Sabrina chuckled. "I know you think he is yummy. I do not think he is yummy, and I really don't want to know about the other parts of his body. He is all yours. But really, I am worried that you are going to get hurt. You like him more than you are letting yourself believe. You forget that he has a girlfriend, and Honey, you are still married." Sabrina paused, and Cheyenne took that time to interrupt.

"Sabrina, calm down. I will be fine. He made it clear that it won't happen again. He kept telling me we can't be doing this, while we were in the middle of it. Besides, I am hoping that it doesn't ruin our friendship. I really do enjoy talking to him."

"I doubt that it will ruin your friendship. He likes you. Anyone who has seen you two together can see it."

"I think you're reading too much into nothing," Cheyenne said. Sabrina was always lecturing her about watching people's body language. She couldn't read people. She would always think one way about something, and it would be the exact opposite.

"I am not. There is a lot of tension between you two. The way you both glow when around each other. The sexual tension is enough to make anyone barf. You think they call you his work wife because of the light bulbs? Please, it is because of the way you two act when you are around each other. He smiles when you walk in the room. He makes special phone calls to the shop for nothing. He likes you. And you like him. You can keep telling yourself that you don't, but everyone sees right through you," she said.

"I'm not sure he likes me the way you think he does. I made the move on him yesterday. I wanted him. I can just look at him, and he can drive me crazy when he answers the phone telling me 'Yo' in his sexy southern accent. All he has to say is that one word and I'm smitten. He drives me crazy when I see him or smell him, and when he smiles at me, I melt. I don't think anyone has ever been able to do that to me. It's messed up. I may like him, but above all else, he is my friend. We will never be more. I know that."

"I think you've already fallen for him, Cheyenne. That is not good."

"Sabrina, we are just friends who happened to have sex once. Amazing sex, that is all."

"Uh huh. Right," she said sarcastically.

"It's the truth. Just one time. I'm about to pull into the driveway and I need to wake up little man. I am going to let you go. I'll text you when I leave in the morning."

"All right. Goodnight."

"Night, Sabrina." Cheyenne hung up the phone. She needed to carry her son in the house without waking him up. She really hoped that she could do it because it was almost 11, and she was tired. She did not want a hyper 4-year-old boy running around the house this late at night.

8

Rolling out of bed the next morning was difficult. Cheyenne felt as if her life had become super complicated overnight. She knew it was her choices that made it feel this way, but she couldn't help believing that her life needed a change soon. She had no idea what she wanted anymore.

She remembered that she was supposed to stop and see Sebastian on her way to the shop. She looked in the mirror and smiled. Just thinking about him brought a smile to her lips. Cheyenne quickly showered and found a pair of jeans to wear with a nice T-shirt. She loved how Sebastian liked the way she looked, no matter what she wore to work. When she first met him, she always wore baggy clothes. He would always say, 'hey don't you look nice,' even when she looked awful. Cheyenne had stopped caring about what she looked like for so many years. It was so nice to feel pretty once again. And it was him who made her feel that way.

She couldn't wait to tell Sebastian the nickname that Sabrina gave to him. She thought it was funny and just hoped that he did, too. She decided to text him, since he should be at work by now. "Sabrina doesn't like calling you my work husband. She decided to pick an emoji, and since I think that you are lick-able, she picked a lollipop emoji. LOL"

It didn't take long for Sebastian to answer her. "Why doesn't she like it?" He asked her.

She was hoping that he wasn't mad. "Beats me, she never really gave me a reasonable answer."

"Maybe she is jealous......." was his reply.

"Jealous of...?"

"US" he said. She was really confused now. Just yesterday Sebastian had made it clear to her there was no 'us,' and now today he claimed there was.

"Could be, no touchy for her. Do you know how badly I want to tell her? Do you have a minute to chat if I stop by?" She asked.

Sebastian's reply was slow coming in. "Not really. The boss is here."

Cheyenne could feel the disappointment creeping in. She really wanted to see him. "That is a bummer," she responded.

His message back to her made her feel better. "I told you, I would be less upset if you told Sabrina rather than telling Jennie."

"Babe, I won't tell her unless you give me the ok. I know you don't like Jennie. I respect that you don't want me to say anything to her. Sabrina figured it out anyway since she knows that I like you, and she did help me go get bras and cute outfits. Besides, I know not to touch you in public and you know that, right?"

"I don't care if you tell her, as long as she can keep quiet...... And yes, I know that." She thought his message sounded as if he might be a little frustrated with her.

Well, she might as well ask him if he is. "Ok. Are you frustrated with me this morning?"

For his boss being there he sure was quick to answer. "No... why?"

"Just asking... Maybe I should frustrate you." She thought for a moment before she sent another text to him. "Have you ever listened to a song that hit close to how you feel?"

"Yup" was his only reply.

"Yeah well... I heard one this morning. And it's got me going crazy! Ugh!"

"What song, Honey?"

"'Addicted to' by Saving Abel. I can send you the words I am talking about." She knew in order to send the words to him she would have to look them up. She didn't have them all memorized.

"K," was all he replied.

"I don't know if you have heard the song before." She waited a few minutes before she googled the words. Cheyenne was sitting at the shop.

It was easy for her to text. She was pretty sure that Sebastian was probably busy at work, and she couldn't wait to call and order parts so she could hear his voice. She found the song lyrics and cut and pasted them into a text message.

�"It's not like you to turn away
All the bullshit I can't take
Just when I think I can walk away,
I'm so addicted to all the things
You do when you're going down on me
In between the sheets
All the sounds you make
With every breathe
It's unlike anything" �

She looked out the window. It was snowing hard. It was hard to believe yesterday was almost 60 degrees and today it was snowing so hard she could barely see the building next door. "Do you see this shit coming down?" She wrote.

"Yup," he replied.

"Did you order this shit?" She asked him. "Oh, and by the way, I guess I'm staying in town on the 27th. I have to be here at the shop by 6 on the 28th.

"Why so early? It's work." Sebastian's replies were short, so she was unsure if he was mad at her. She didn't think she did anything to make him mad, but it's possible. She knew that sometimes her mouth spoke before her brain had time to catch up. Her lack of a verbal filter got her into trouble daily.

"My mom is having heart surgery and Dad needs my Jeep to take her. He also needs me to sit at the shop all day for him."

"Oh." His reply was simple, and he wasn't exactly helping her with carrying on a conversation.

"I'm trying to figure out this stupid key on a car. It is driving me crazy."

"Slide it in and turn it, Silly," Sebastian said.

"Got to have a hole to do that, Dear." She sent him a picture of the key fob that was sitting on her computer. Cheyenne could only get the key to work if it was in a certain spot in the car, which wasn't supposed to be how the key fob worked. She hit send on her phone and within seconds the shop phone was ringing.

Cheyenne looked over to the caller ID. She saw it was Sebastian's work. She picked up the phone. "Yes, Dear?"

"Honey, what is going on with the key? Maybe I can help you."

"Well, the car will only start if the key fob is in a little holder inside of the middle glove box. I have tried changing the batteries. I have tried both key fobs. I YouTubed it, and I tried the suggestions on there. Nothing seems to work. I just want this car out of here."

"What kind of car is it?" Sebastian asked.

"It's a Ford Taurus. I'm like about to say fuck it and let the junk yard come and get the damned thing."

"Ahh Honey, calm down. We will figure it out. Call down to the Ford dealership and talk to them. Tell them I told you to go there. They can test the key fob and help you figure it out. I'll call down first because I know them, and they probably won't charge you."

"Thank you. I'm beginning to think this idea of taking over my dad's shop is a mistake. I can't seem to figure out any of this stuff. I feel like I'm stupid. I can't even figure out the computer to order parts from you. Maybe this is a bad idea." Cheyenne sighed.

"You are not stupid. There is a lot to learn, and you will have to give yourself some time. You won't be able to do it all overnight. It will be ok. I will be here the whole time, and I will always be here to help you. Give me about 5 minutes to call the Ford Dealership and then you call them. All right?"

"Ok. Thank you." No matter the mood Cheyenne was in, Sebastian could always make her feel better. It was a great feeling to know that he was always there for her and always would be.

They hung up, and she waited like she was supposed to do. Then, she made the call to the Ford dealership. When she got to the parts department, she told the gentleman who answered that Sebastian had told her to call. He told her to bring the keys down and he would test them. He also told her some things to check in the car, which could be the reason the keys were not functioning properly.

"All right, thank you. I'll be up in the next hour. Thank you again for your time."

"No problem," he replied.

She hung up the phone and called Sebastian back at work. His booming voice echoed through the phone. "Yo!"

"I am going to run out to the dealership. The guy said he would test these key fobs. I was checking to see if you wanted anything to eat or drink since I was going to be coming that way."

"I'm not hungry, but could you grab me some tea?"

"Yeah, you want a sweet tea or a flavored tea?"

"Sweet tea with a lid. Please."

"Yep, I'll drop it off after I have the keys checked."

"Thank you. I've got to go; the phones are ringing. See you in a bit." Sebastian hung up without saying goodbye.

~~~~~

Cheyenne walked into Automotive Parts Unlimited, and she smiled when she saw Sebastian at the register closest to the door. She liked it when he was at that register because she could see behind the counter. She could see all of him. He looked up as she approached him. "Hey," she said.

"Hey." He smiled as he spoke. She could feel her cheeks turning red. All he had to do was smile at her and she would melt. His smile made her forget the world around them. It was just him and her, alone.

They both just stared at each other for a moment, until D.J., one of the drivers said, "You two just need to get a room." D.J. was always teasing them and telling them they just needed to get a room and get it over with. D.J. was a tall, slender man, about six-two. Cheyenne guessed he was in his 50s, though she wasn't sure of his actual age. He had grayish-blond hair and a mouth like a sailor. Sebastian and D.J. were always at each other's throats. The two never got along, which is why Sebastian always
~~~~~

referred to him as "Big Stoopie." Sebastian was always telling Cheyenne that he was going to stab him. He had even threatened once.

"Shut up, D.J. Don't you have something to do with your life? Like maybe your job?" Cheyenne spatted at D.J. Some days she couldn't stand him. He didn't say anything back to her. He just walked away. "I brought your tea," she said in a soft, calm voice. She just watched him while fiddling with the sleeve to her black hoodie. She was nervous around him today and she wasn't sure why. Cheyenne admired how he looked in his black work attire.

"Thank you," he said as his phone rang. He answered, "Yup, Charlie, he just left with the alternator about 5 minutes ago. He should be there any minute." Sebastian watched Cheyenne as he spoke. "Yep, thanks, Charlie."

"Can you go out and smoke?" She asked him after he hung up the phone.

"I can't right now. If you come out later, I can take a smoke break. I have a lot to do today. We received a lot of orders from the weekend that still need processed." His phone started to ring again.

"I'll talk to you later." She didn't wait for a response, she just turned and walked out the door and headed back to the shop. As soon as she pulled into the shop, she sent him a message. "Sorry I just left. You're super busy. Talk to you later, Babe." Sebastian did not message her the rest of the day. Around 4:30 p.m. she decided to see if he was mad at her. "Did I make you mad?" She waited a while and never got an answer. She had no idea what happened but figured she'd better finish her day and head home to her kid. The ride home was long... she was worried that one evening ruined her relationship with someone who was her best friend. When she was on her way home, he finally answered.

"Not mad; I was busy. What are you doing?" Sebastian asked.

"Just left town and headed home. What are you doing?" The rest of the night was quiet. She didn't hear anything else from him.

~~~~~

The next day at the shop she texted him again. She sent her normal
~~~~~

morning text. Nothing back from him all day. She had no reason to call the parts store, since they didn't need any parts, and he made no effort to call the shop like he would normally do.

She finished the day and headed home. She was so confused about what was going on, and she was starting to get annoyed with him. Just as she was getting ready to call Jennie, her phone rang. She sang the words to the ring tone for a moment. "I'm so addicted to the things you do." She smiled because that was Sebastian's new ringtone. "What!" she answered, trying to sound annoyed with him.

"Now, Honey, that is not a nice way to answer the phone." Sebastian's voice rang through the phone.

"Well... You have ignored me all day. So, excuse me if I'm a little upset." Cheyenne said, trying to get her anger under control.

"Honey, I'm sorry, but we were really busy. I didn't have time to text you. Then when I got home her kid was here, so, I had to wait for her to leave to call you. Don't be mad..." He trailed off.

"I'm not mad. I thought you were mad at me, after the weekend," she said. "I thought you were going to stop talking to me. Hang on a moment... Never mind, I will call you right back."

"Ok. Well, I might be busy by then. So, I might not answer."

"Well, if you don't answer then I guess we won't talk tonight," Cheyenne said as she hung up the phone. She was really becoming pissed off. There was no way he was so busy that he couldn't take two seconds to text her and say he was busy.

She stopped at the gas station and fueled up her Jeep before calling him back. When she did, it rang and rang. She figured he didn't answer on purpose, likely trying to control the situation. It wasn't very long before he called her back. She was so tempted to decline the call, but Sebastian had a way with her, and she knew it. She had a hard time ignoring his calls. When they had a disagreement, if she saw him, he would smile, and she was unable to stay mad at him for long. She felt like he was her kryptonite.

"Hello, sorry, Babe. I had to stop and get gas, and I had to pee." She said as she answered the phone.

"Right..." was all he managed to say.

"Boy, what is your problem?"

"Nothing, apparently just a boy here," Sebastian snapped.

"Really, you are getting mad over being called a boy? It's better than 'dude,' but whatever."

"No, it's not," he retorted.

"You know what? Whatever, Sebastian. All I wanted to do was talk to you. I love listening to your stories and talking to you, but if you don't want to talk to me then whatever. You do you from now on." Cheyenne knew she was going to regret what she said, but she said it anyway and hung up the phone. After she hung up, she sent him a text. "If you want to text, fine; if not, fine. Topic is on you."

She pulled into her driveway, grabbed her things, and headed into the house. She doubted he would answer her. He seemed to be with one of his friends and three sheets to the wind. When she walked in the house, there were no kids to be seen, but there was a note on the counter from her husband.

Hey, the kids and I are down at the neighbors. Come down if you want. We will be home later.

Cheyenne slipped her shoes off and grabbed her slippers. She changed into her pajamas and headed to her office to write and relax in her chair. She had an old rocking chair that she got from the daycare from when she used to work there. The chair was worn out and then some, but it was her special place to sit and think in the dark.

Finally, he replied to her: "You the one that wants to text a boy... what you got?" Now she could really tell he was drunk because normally he was a stickler when it came to grammar

"What? Say that again, Dear." She could only imagine what the reply would be.

"What you got.... Just a boy asking..." She had two options – just ignore his ignorance and continue the text or get mad and go off on him.

"Well, you're at least a handsome boy," she said, adding a kissy emoji at the end. "What I got hmmm. I'm sitting in my office in the dark..."

"Humm, so what are the big plans for Saturday?" He asked.

"It's a surprise. You'll have to let me take you out and spoil you."

"I don't know.... The stripper from last night has been texting me," he said with a cocky attitude again.

By now Cheyenne was done trying to talk to him. He had really pissed her off. "Ok. Have fun!"

"Really... I expected more out of that one," he replied.

"What do you want me to say? Do I want you to sleep with someone else? Nope, sure don't. But..." She took a deep breath before she sent the rest of what she wanted to say. "I don't own you, Babe. Are you trying to make me jealous?"

"Nope... Just playing with you," he replied.

"Are you sure? I think you like it when I get all riled up."

"Nothing to get riled up about," he insisted. She rolled her eyes at his answer.

"I'm not sure what you're wanting me to say."

"Not wanting you to say anything. I'm doing me, tonight," he said.

"No shit! Are you picking a fight? I don't want to fight with you. You want to go fuck a stripper, GO YOU! I don't own you, Sebastian. You are a grown-ass man; you will do you. Do I want you to? NO! But it's not my choice. It's yours!" She hit send and didn't give him a chance to reply before she sent more. "I'm going to get ready to go for a run... If you decide to stop being a jerk, give me a call. Or even text. But if you want to continue to be a jerk and hurt my feelings, then don't bother doing either!" She got up out of her chair, put on her running gear, and headed next door to the cemetery to go for a run.

When she returned, she took a shower and got ready for bed. To her surprise, there was a message from Sebastian. "Goodnight, Honey. Talk to you tomorrow." She didn't know if she should even answer him, but she knew deep down inside she had to. She wanted to. She needed to.

"Night." She replied. She wanted to say more. She was afraid if she did then he would start being a jerk again.

9

The next morning Sebastian texted her like normal. He acted like nothing had happened the night before. Over the next few days everything seemed to get back to normal.

She was sitting in the shop with her feet propped up on the desk when Sabrina walked in. "What are you doing tonight, lady?" She asked Cheyenne.

"I'm not really sure. Why, what's up?"

"The kid and I were going to go to dinner and wanted to see if you wanted to come. I thought you said your husband had the kids for the night. And I need to talk to you," Sabrina said in a pleading tone.

"Sure. I won't be done for another hour. You want to come and get me then?" Cheyenne asked.

"Okie dokie. We will be back. Later!" She waved and walked out the door. It didn't seem very long after Sabrina left that Sebastian walked into the shop. Cheyenne didn't notice until she heard him say something because she was engrossed in paperwork, lost in her own thoughts.

"Hey, Honey. Where's your daddy?" Sebastian asked, standing in the doorway of the office. "I have a question for him."

She looked up. "He's in the shop." She smiled at him when he smiled his special smile for her.

"Thanks," he said as he walked over and put a Twisted Tea in the fridge and took one of the cold ones with him to talk to her dad. As much as she wanted to go out to the shop with her dad and Sebastian, she knew she had work to do.

As time slowly ticked by, Cheyenne got her work done. Sabrina returned with a child in tow to help finish work so they could go to dinner. The last 30 minutes slowed to an even more excruciating crawl. It was like waiting to watch water come to a boil in front of them. When the shop closed, they heaved a sigh of relief and turned their attention to getting things put away. They then waited on Sebastian and Cheyenne's father to end their talk. Sebastian kept sneaking peeks at Cheyenne. She just watched him, leaning against the red truck they were all standing by. Cheyenne was ready to go but had to wait until her dad was ready to go so, they could all head out for the night.

The restaurant was across town from the shop, just past where Sebastian worked. "I wish Sebastian would come eat with us," Cheyenne said to Sabrina.

"Call and ask him."

"You can. He'll say no. He won't go anywhere in public with me because he doesn't want to get caught."

"He can say this is a business dinner. I bet you I can get him to come out here and eat," Sabrina said.

"I doubt it. I'll take that bet because I know he won't come," Cheyenne said. She knew he wouldn't come out here no matter what they offered him.

"Well, call him and hand me the phone," Sabrina said.

Cheyenne opened her phone and clicked his name. The phone rang and she doubted Sebastian would pick up, but he surprised her. "Hey, Honey," he answered.

"Hey, Sabrina wants to talk to you."

"Ok," he said. She handed the phone to Sabrina.

"Hello. So, we have an idea. You should come out to Perkins and have dinner with us." She was quiet for a moment. Cheyenne assumed she was listening to him. "Cheyenne, he wants to know what he will get if he comes out here..." Cheyenne rolled her eyes. "He said don't roll your eyes at him."

"How the hell does he know I rolled my eyes? Tell him we will think of something," Cheyenne said.

"Sebastian, we bet on whether or not you would come to dinner with us. Cheyenne says that you won't, and I said you would. Don't make me lose the bet. Come out and eat dinner with us." Sabrina and Sebastian talked for a few moments before she handed the phone back to Cheyenne.

"Yes, Dear," she said.

"I have things to do. I can't come out right now. Besides, I don't really like their food. Call me when you're done eating and I'll meet you somewhere."

"Ok," Cheyenne said. She was trying not to show disappointment in her voice. "I'll talk to you in a bit then. Bye."

"Honey, don't be mad."

"I'm not mad. It's all right."

"Ok. I'll talk to you in a bit. Bye," he said. She hung up the phone.

"Told you he wouldn't come," she told Sabrina. They were both quiet for a while. Their dinner was casual; Cheyenne and Sabrina talked about texting Sebastian while Sabrina's child played on her phone.

The bustle of the restaurant was slowly picking up, and they watched the staff scurry from table to table. Cheyenne decided to text Sebastian. "So, Sabrina wants to stalk you. She says she is joking, but I don't think so. You could have three stalkers."

"I told you I think she is hot, right?" Sebastian responded to Cheyenne.

"Yes Dear, am I supposed to be jealous? Wish you would come eat with us. Pretty sure we didn't bet on that. And I'm pretty sure her name wasn't brought up."

"I guess that was a no... I did bring her up." He replied.

"You said you liked her hair and then went to her being hot, I think. Just saying. Before we leave you should take five minutes to come see us. You never answered my question from earlier."

"What was that?"

"Did you look through our texts?" She asked him. Cheyenne gave him a minute to think before she sent another message. She just sent two words. "Ultimate fantasy?"

All he sent back was, "No Jealousy."

"Oh, I'm not jealous, Doll. I don't own you. Do I want to fuck the shit out of you? Yes! Own you, no."

"That's good...... I already told you how I think the ripping the clothes is so very hot."

"Yes, but you don't have any spare clothes with you, do you?" She asked.

"That's probably the ultimate...."

"What's 'good,' by the way?" She asked.

"Ownership..." he said.

"Nothing on the other? LOL." She probed, and then she showed Sabrina the messages.

"Ask him if he's for sale." Sabrina told Cheyenne. They both giggled.

"Are you for sale?" She asked Sebastian.

"If the price is right..."

"What is the price? You never answered me on the position." She said to him.

"I told you its situational... And a lot." Sebastian said. Earlier in the week Cheyenne and Sebastian had been playing 20. She asked what was his favorite sexual position. The only thing he would say in his answer was it is situational.

"Yes, I'm aware. Bed? Or hood? And how much money is a lot? Sabrina says to answer her message." Cheyenne wasn't sure what they were talking about, but she had a feeling that Sabrina was being a good wingman.

"Did I mention that I have things to do?" Sebastian said.

Cheyenne giggled; she knew that Sabastian wasn't getting anything done with them both texting him. "A few times.... Did I mention that I'm a pain in the ass...? I can stop bothering you."

"Now she has me going on pie..." He replied.

She was very confused. She wanted to ask Sabrina what they were talking about... But if she wanted her to know she would tell her. She responded, "Pie?"

"I don't like the pie they serve at Perkins.... Just saying..."

"Pretty sure that is not the conversation...... Just saying..."

"Well, it was but my mind.... Wheels turning and all." He wrote back.

She knew now that he was now trying to make her jealous. "Stop thinking about her muffin... Problem solved." She wrote. She had to think long and hard about her answers; she didn't want him to know that she was a little bit jealous of Sabrina.

The waitress came to their table. "How are things going? Is there anything else I can get you?"

"Yes, we need your input... Our friend doesn't like pie and we are joking with him, and we want to get him something, just to be smart asses. Do you have a suggestion?" Sabrina said.

"I have an idea. I will be right back." The waitress scurried off.

"What do you think her idea is?" Cheyenne asked Sabrina.

"I have no idea." Sabrina said, shrugging her shoulders.

After a few minutes the waitress came back with a muffin. "Here's an apple pie muffin, since you guys are teasing him." Cheyenne and Sabrina started giggling.

"That will be perfect. Thank you!" Cheyenne said. They paid their bill and then the three girls piled into Sabrina's car, apple pie muffin in hand, all because Sebastian didn't like pie. "Let me call him to make sure it's safe to stop there." She opened her phone and clicked his name.

"Yo," he answered.

Cheyenne giggled, "So we got you something and we want to drop it off. Is it safe to stop by? And no, it's not pie."

"Yeah, you can."

"Ok, we will see you in a few." She hung up the phone. They arrived at his home a short time later, and he was standing in the driveway when they pulled in.

Cheyenne was giggling as she handed him the bag with the muffin. Their hands touched, and he slowly pulled his hand away, running his fingers over hers. The feeling sent chills up her arms.

"Since you don't like pie, we got you an apple pie muffin... they didn't have any cupcakes," Sabrina said. "You have to try it." She paused. "Like now, so we know it's good."

Sebastian took the muffin out of the bag and took a bit of the caramel from the top. In doing so he got caramel all over his fingers. He looked straight at Cheyenne, staring into her eyes, and licked each finger slowly, putting the whole finger in his mouth and sucking on it. Watching Sebastian made her warm inside, and the coil in her belly tightened.

"It's pretty good," he said. Cheyenne wasn't sure whether he really liked it, or if he was just saying that to make her feel good. "You know, texting you two is like texting one brain. Girls, I'd really love to chat, but I do have things to do."

"Ok, we will text you," Cheyenne said.

"I will answer when I can," Sebastian said. "Have a good night, girls. Don't get into any trouble."

"We won't," Sabrina said as she started to back out of the driveway.

Cheyenne's car was broken down so Sabrina said she would give her a ride home. They headed out of town; Cheyenne lived about an hour away from them. She decided to send Sebastian a message about what he said about them having one brain. "If talking to us is like talking to two people with one Brian, isn't having sex with one of us having sex with both of us?" She asked him. "Just saying."

"Actually, I was thinking about yours...... and who is Brian?" He replied.

"I think you like Sabrina. Autocorrect. Damn it! I was using voice-to-text," she said. "Mine?" Cheyenne didn't realize at first that he was talking about her sexual muffin.

"Yes," came his response.

"Why?"

"Why not... I am a perv..."

"Ummm. I don't think I follow, right now. Explain...." She responded to him.

"Muffins... if they are warm, hot and a little sticky, yum... Usually the cream is at the bottom end and not on the top."

"Must have been sticky... Having to lick fingers..." She replied to him. "Well, my dear. If lick you, what should I." Cheyenne didn't know it at the time but her autocorrect on her phone changed the whole sentence. "It should have said, 'If I can't lick you what can I lick?'

"Ok, enough... both of you... now I am having thoughts of caramel and cream running through my head." Sebastian said.

"She's the caramel and I'm the cream. You didn't answer the question." She sent him a pouty emoji at the end.

"What question?" He answered.

"The licking..." She replied.

"Wasn't really a question. Reread it....it really wasn't a statement either..."

Cheyenne was starting to get mad at her phone. It was changing her words. "Damn autocorrect. If I can't lick you, what can I lick? My fucking phone is going to get thrown."

"What is the matter, Cheyenne? You look mad." Cheyenne looked up from her phone and over at Sabrina.

"No, I'm not mad at him. My phone keeps changing my words. It is making me angry."

"Oh, I hate autocorrect. It does it to me, too. Then you're like 'how did you even get that from what I was saying?'" They both started to giggle. Cheyenne stopped when her phone went off again.

"All right.... you two have caused enough trouble for one day... talk to you more in the morning," Sebastian wrote.

Cheyenne started to feel bummed out. He didn't want to talk anymore. She decided to send one more message. "What trouble have we caused?...So no licking. :(."

"Suckers, honey... talk to you two tomorrow." Sebastian said. She was unsure why he was bringing up suckers when she was talking about licking him.

Cheyenne decided she would text until he stopped texting. "Ok. Not as fun..."

"What's not?"

"Lots of reasons. Not as tasty..." she replied. She was unsure if she knew that he she wasn't wanting to suck on a sucker. She wanted to lick him.

"Lost," he sent back to her.

"Suckers don't taste as good and don't do anything for ya..." Cheyenne responded.

"Sometimes the "sucker" does do it for you...... Goodnight."

"It doesn't wiggle or squirm when I lick it. Or make cute moaning noises." Cheyenne said before saying, "night."

Sebastian was quick to respond: "Wrong sucker, Honey."

Now Cheyenne felt stupid. She had no idea what he was talking about. "WTF man, I'm so confused."

"Think about it - sucker... or suckie," he replied. Now she got it. He was talking about sucking on him, not on a sucker itself.

"Mmmhmmm permission?" She asked him.

"For?" was his only response.

"Licking your lollipop?" She asked.

"Not saying no... got to go." He replied.

"When, where and I'm game.... Goodnight."

~~~~

Cheyenne woke the next morning to a text from Sabrina. "Louis found out about me texting Sebastian. He is uber mad at me. I don't know what to do. What should I do?"

"I don't know what you should do. What did you two talk about that was so bad?" Cheyenne asked.

"We talked about you, and he told me I was hot, and I told him no way, that I was happy with Louis. I can send you what he sent me. We talked about you some, but not a lot." Sabrina replied.

"Send me the messages, and I'll read them when I get to the shop." After she arrived at work, she read through the messages. So many of the messages were him hitting on her, and her hitting on him. She could see why Louis would be mad. She didn't make it clear until the end of the texting that she was happy with her boyfriend. Cheyenne was kind of angry about the way he was talking to her.

She sent Sabrina a message. "So is Louis talking to you at all?"

"No, he told me I was cheating on him and he couldn't deal with me. I can't live without him. I can't eat; I feel so sick."

"Where are you?" Cheyenne asked Sabrina.
~~~~

"Work, but I can't stay here. I'm going to go home."

"Go home and take a nap. Then come here when you wake up."

"Ok. I will."

"Everything will be fine. I'll message Sebastian and tell him you can't talk to him for now. Then I will message Louis and see if I can tell him you were messaging him for me. Or that it was me messaging him."

"Ok thank you."

Cheyenne went to send a message to Sebastian, but he beat her to it. "Sabrina said that she is in trouble with her boyfriend for texting me."

"Ya, she told me it was because he considers it cheating," Cheyenne said. "I'll figure it out and let you know," she added.

"Sounds good. I'll talk to you later," Sebastian replied.

Cheyenne started working on paperwork and cleaning the office. She spent most of the day scraping the bathroom to get it ready to paint. She didn't hear much from Sabrina until the afternoon. She figured she was still sleeping.

Finally, 5 o'clock rolled around and Cheyenne was ready to leave. She hadn't heard from Sabrina all day. She decided to send her a text. "You awake? Was going to stop by."

"Yes, I'm awake. Let me know when you're on your way here," Sabrina messaged back.

"Leaving the shop now," Cheyenne said. She was leaving as Sebastian was pulling into the shop. She stopped for a moment to say hi to him.

"Are you leaving?" He asked her. Cheyenne just stared at him; he was wearing shorts. It was nice out, but she didn't feel like it was that nice. His legs were muscular. She couldn't get over how nice he looked.

"Umm, yeah. I'm going to go check on Sabrina," Cheyenne finally answered. She felt so out of place. She wasn't planning on seeing him today. She wore a pair of baggy pants and a T-shirt. Her hair was up in a bun that didn't quite cover up the paint chips stuck in her hair. She smiled at him, and he smiled back. He had a special smile that he gave only to her. His grin made all her worries disappear. She could get lost in his smile.

She was unsure how long they stood there before he broke the awkward silence. "Is your daddy still here?" She could never understand why he always called him her daddy and not just her dad. It made her feel like a small child.

"Ya, he's inside. I'm not sure what he's doing. He's supposed to be doing brake lines, but he hasn't touched the truck yet. Call me when you leave here."

"Ok," he said as he headed toward the front door to the shop.

Cheyenne climbed into her Jeep and headed towards Sabrina's house. When she arrived, Sabrina was sitting on the steps crying and drinking some sort of drink. When Cheyenne parked in the driveway, Sabrina came over to the car and climbed into the front seat.

She didn't say anything at first, but you could see that she was crying. "Did you take a nap?" Cheyenne asked her.

"No, I have been trying to get him to talk to me. He said he hated me." Sabrina started to sob again.

"He doesn't hate you. He is just mad at the situation. He probably feels threatened by the thought of you talking to another man. Even if you were doing it for me. Men don't rationalize, they just act," Cheyenne explained.

"You don't think he hates me?" Sabrina said looking up at Cheyenne.

"No, he doesn't hate you. And to be honest, he shouldn't be mad. He has texted other girls before and still does, which is no different. Besides, that other girl was trying to get in his pants. I don't think that Sebastian was necessarily trying to get in your pants. I think he knew you would show me, and I believe that he is trying to make me jealous."

"I'm sure he was because he wasn't getting a reaction out of you. I offered to let Louis read the messages, but he wouldn't even do that. He told me he didn't need to because it's still cheating. What am I going to do?"

"You are going to do nothing. You are going to stop texting him. It is a control thing. He has no right to treat you like that. You go inside and take care of his kid. Then when he comes home you go to bed and ignore him. Give him the same treatment he has given you."

Sabrina was quiet for a moment before she spoke. "I don't know if I can do that, not talk to him. Knowing he is mad at me makes me sick to my stomach. I feel lost and confused without him."

"You can do it. I have faith that you can do it. I will talk to you my whole drive home. Then, until you fall asleep. Ok?"

"Ok," Sabrina said.

"If you are ok, I'm going to head home to my kids. I told them that I would be home early tonight," Cheyenne said, as if seeking permission to go ahead and leave.

"Yeah, I think I'll be ok. I am going to go in and make supper and go to bed.

"All right, call me or text me if you need me," Cheyenne said as Sabrina climbed out of the Jeep.

10

Cheyenne finally made it home. She had gone for her nightly run, mainly to clear her head. She came home and showered, and by that time she figured she would have heard from Sebastian, but his girlfriend must have been home. She always had to ruin all her fun. Cheyenne was just about to crawl into bed when her phone started to ring. She looked down and saw it was Sabrina. “Hello,” she said with a yawn.

“I can’t do this. I'm sitting here staring at a knife. I just want to end my life. He said he’s never talking to me again. Cheyenne, what do I do?”

“Here's what you're going to do. First, you are going to put the knife away. Next you are going to pack some clothes and I am going to come get you; we can get a hotel room for a few days. That way, you guys can have some space. How does that sound?”

“Ok. Can we leave as soon as he gets here to be with his daughter? Will you be here before he arrives?” She asked.

“Yes, I should be. Let me throw some clothes in a bag and let the hubby know what's going on. Then I'll head out. I'll call the hotel and make a room reservation.”

“Cheyenne, I don’t have any money to pay for a room. Are you going to stay with me? Or are you going to go back home?”

“I can stay with you, if you want me to. I can pay for it. Hey, what are friends for?”

“I do. Thank you. Will you let me know when you leave?”

“Yep, I sure will.” Cheyenne hung up the phone. She went to explain the whole situation to her husband and then threw some clothes in an overnight bag and grabbed her work shoes and everything she needed. She told everyone she would be back and gave her son a kiss. She hopped in her Jeep and started the hour-long drive to Sabrina's house. She was already tired of being in the car. All she wanted to do was go to sleep.

Upon arrival at Sabrina's house, she found her friend sitting outside with a bag of things, a blanket, and a few pillows. "We can't leave until he pulls in the driveway, so I don't leave his kid alone," Sabrina said.

"All right, how long until he gets here?" Cheyenne asked, yawning. "I have the room booked. Two days away should help." It wasn't long after Cheyenne had arrived at Sabrina's, when Louis pulled up to the house. He was a bigger guy and very well built. He had fire-red hair, but it was dyed black, and he was a hair taller than Cheyenne.

Louis got out of his car and stormed into the house. Sabrina followed him in. She wasn't in there long when she came back outside crying. She got in the car. "I'm ready to go." The drive to the hotel was quiet, and Cheyenne respected the fact that Sabrina did not want to talk.

Cheyenne checked them into the hotel. Sabrina followed her up the stairs and down the hall toward the room, walking like she was headed towards her own demise. Once Cheyenne opened the door, Sabrina walked into the room and flopped down on the bed, exhaling in a huge sigh. The room was nice, with two queen-size beds. Each bed was made up with bright, white sheets, and there was a small desk in the corner near the window. Cheyenne had stayed in this hotel before, and it was one of her favorites.

Sabrina had brought a few wine coolers, and each of them opened one and sat on their own beds and drank in silence. Nothing needed to be said. Cheyenne knew what was going through Sabrina's mind. If she wanted to talk about the situation she would. She wasn't about to force her to talk if she was not ready.

Cheyenne knew it was late, but she sent a message to Sebastian. "Umm problem..." She knew he wouldn't answer until morning, but she wanted to give him a heads-up. She didn't say much because she knew that if his girlfriend got hold of his phone, he could pretend the message was from the wrong number.

She was unsure how long they sat there sipping on the wine cooler before she decided to break the silence. "Sabrina if you want to stay up, we can, but I am ready to go to sleep. I have to work in the morning. You can do what you want while I'm gone tomorrow."

No, we don't have to stay up; I'm tired, too. We can go to sleep. Well, at least I'll try."

~~~~

Cheyenne felt as if the next morning came way too early. It was 6:30, and she needed to get up and shower. She really wanted to go for a quick run, but she could barely keep her eyes open from having to pick up Sabrina so late. She realized she was no longer one who could stay up all night.

When she got out of the shower, got dressed, and emerged from the bathroom, Sabrina was sitting up in her bed. "Hey," she said.

"Hey, yourself! Did you get any sleep?" Cheyenne asked.

"A little. Louis and I talked most of the night. He said he wanted to talk this morning. He is coming here after you go to work."

"Oh," was the only response Cheyenne could muster. She was angry because she knew she'd take him back. She always forgave him even when he was wrong. When she was about to get up and leave, she received a text from Sebastian.

"What is the problem?" Sebastian asked.

"I'm so tired. She's making me angry already."

"Why? Isn't she trying to pull you back into bed? That would make me so very angry" Sebastian said. How did he know where she was and who she was with? Maybe he had seen her Jeep and just figured.

"Why are you angry, and maybe?" Cheyenne sat on the bed beside Sabrina and they sent him a selfie of them cuddling. Cheyenne knew it would get him going.

"Aww... Is that how you two slept last night?" He asked.

"What happens in the hotel stays in the hotel.... Definitely cuddles..." Cheyenne added; she knew she would be able to tease him for once instead of the other way around.
~~~~

"Could have at least taken a couple of pictures for me." She could read the disappointment in his text message.

"Sorry, I promised her no pictures and no Facebook posting." She was hoping that one got him. Since he wouldn't let her have pictures of them when he was with her in the hotel room. At the end of her message, she sent him the kissy-face emoji.

"That's no fun!" Sebastian answered. Both of the girls were giggling as Cheyenne responded to the message:

"Well... I am all for negotiating on this topic."

"I don't care about Facebook, so I'm good with just pictures," he answered. He didn't get her reference about what he said to her the night they were together.

Cheyenne thought for a moment before she answered him. "What are your offers? Put your cards on the table dear...."

"What do you two demons want in trade?" He replied. Sabrina and Cheyenne giggled at his reply.

"You go to dinner with us......."

"Where and when? And no kids." Sebastian responded within seconds of Cheyenne's message.

"Well... She would have to find a sitter if she cannot bring the kid with her."

Cheyenne smiled at his response. "I guess that kind of P.G.'s things...."

"Kinda, the kid can go down to the pool." Cheyenne suggested.

"She's with you now?" He asked.

"The kid? No, she's at school."

"So now would be a good time for pictures!" Cheyenne laughed out loud when she read his message. There was no way she was falling for that one.

"Oh, no way! You have to hold up your end first." She sent a picture of Sabrina lying in the bed beside her. She was wearing a red hoodie and Minion pajama pants. She was flipping him off in the picture. Then she sent another message: "Best you get this a.m."

She started laughing harder with his reply. "That's not very nice!"

"Never claimed to be nice..."

"I guess not," he replied. She wondered if he was feigning to pout.

"Honestly, have I ever said I was nice? Nope, I haven't. You just assumed." She giggled to herself. "Do you want to stop?"

"I can't stop, Honey, I'm at work," he responded.

"No, us there." She wrote after she realized that she left a word out of her last message.

"That's fine."

She got up and headed towards the door. "Are you staying here then, to wait for Louis?"

"Yeah. I'll let you know what we decide to do."

"All right, talk to you later." Cheyenne rolled her eyes as she turned towards the door.

"Bye," Sabrina said as Cheyenne walked out of the room. She walked downstairs and out to the parking lot. She only had to drive from one parking lot to the other. She could walk but wanted to be lazy today.

When she got to his work, she pulled into her normal parking spot. She parked where Sebastian always stood to smoke. She really didn't know why she did, but she always parked in the same space. She grabbed her phone out of her pocket and sent him another message. "Do I have to come in there?"

He didn't answer her. But, when she looked up, he was standing by the door waiting to let her in, since the store wasn't open yet. He was sporting that "get your ass in here" look, so she just smiled and took her sweet time walking to the door. As she got closer to the entrance, he started to break into a grin. She followed him inside. Sebastian walked over to the counter, picked up a Rice Krispy bar and started to eat it slowly. She rolled her eyes at him, which made him smile.

"Well, are you going to tell me what happened?" Sebastian asked, as he continued to get the shop ready for the day.

Cheyenne hopped up on the tool counter. She loved to sit up there. "Yeah. Well, I had to go pick her up because her and her boyfriend got into a fight over you. He called her a whore and told her she was cheating on him with you. I tried to message him and said that it was me messaging instead of her, but that didn't help any. Just made him madder at her."

"So, you lied to him and said it was you texting me or, was it really you?" Sebastian asked as he raised an eyebrow at her. "Hmmm?"

"Well, I lied to him. I didn't know what she was saying to you most of the time. It was a private text between you two. I only know now because she sent them all to me when she got in trouble. I didn't want to lie, but I didn't want the conversation between the two of you to ruin her relationship." She paused for a moment and folded her arms over her chest. "Did I like your text to her? No, but you're not mine, and I don't own you, so you can say what you want. You can talk to whomever you want."

Sebastian just changed the subject. "Thought she was coming with you."

"Nope, her boyfriend is on his way to the hotel. So, they can talk, I guess." Cheyenne shrugged her shoulders. "I don't know what is going on anymore."

"I see," he said, as he went to unlock the door. There were cars already in the parking lot.

"I'd better get going to the shop. I'll text you," she said as she hopped off the counter.

"All right. Bye," he said as he waved to her.

"Bye," she said, waving back at him before heading towards the door. Before pushing the door open, she stopped and looked back at him. He was helping someone get parts. He looked over at her and suddenly she felt her face turn red. He must have known she was checking him out because he just smiled his special smile for her.

As she walked towards her Jeep, she was really wishing she didn't have to work today. She would love to have sat there and watched him all day.

Once she was in her Jeep, she sent him a quick message. "I'm hurt, mad. I haven't ever lied to you. I'm a very honest person." She was unsure if he would answer her. He was getting busy at work, and it was just him there, for now.

She headed to the shop. Her dad was already there. She went into the office and started to open everything up. Cheyenne was so tired; tired enough that her stomach was starting to flop.

It was a slow morning. She decided to send Sebastian another text. "I need chocolate."

Whenever Sebastian messaged her back, she could practically hear his voice. She smiled when her phone went off. "I'll send you some."

"Hmm."

She looked up from her phone as someone was walking into the office. It was Jennie. "What's up?" She asked.

"Nothing. How about you?" Cheyenne was sitting with her black Nike hoodie pulled up over her head. She was sporting blue jeans and her postal boots. She was freezing.

Jennie must have had to go to work when she left the shop. She was wearing her DQ uniform. "Are you going to tell me what happened between Dumb and Dumber?" Jennie didn't care for Sabrina. And, she cared even less for Louis. She didn't like how he treated her as if he owned her.

"Not much to tell. She was texting Sebastian and her boyfriend found out and flipped. Some of the messages might have gone too far. But Sebastian is a perv sometimes so... I really have no excuse for either of them. He told me he thought she was hot."

"Yuck! She is not hot. You are way hotter than her. Did you see the messages?"

"Yeah, she sent them to me. He kind of made me mad. He didn't want me to know they were still texting at 10 last night. And, I feel like she may have deleted some of the messages because she told me she told him to eat in front of me and such. And those messages were not in the conversation."

"Well, I think she likes him. I can tell by the way she dresses when he's around," Jennie said. "Besides, she knows you like him, sooo, there's that."

"I'd think since she knows that I like him she would not even go there," Cheyenne said.

"Well, you don't have to worry about me going there because that is NEVER going to happen. I already told you that I think you need to walk away from this one. Remember I know his ex-wife and I have known him for a long time. But I respect that you like him, and I'll attempt to be nice to him." She paused as she leaned back in the chair across from Cheyenne. "Maybe... I'll be nice to him. If he hurts you, I'm going to hurt him," she said.

Cheyenne knew that Jennie wasn't kidding. She hated Sebastian with a passion. "I know you'll hurt him, but I appreciate you being nice to him, I really do."

"I have to get to work. I'll stop afterwards." Jennie stood and headed toward the door.

"Ok. I'll talk to you later. If you have time, call me on your break." Cheyenne said as she answered the phone.

Cheyenne looked up from her paperwork to her dad standing in front of her. "Call and order some oil dry. Tell him you want the good stuff."

"Ok," she said as she grabbed her cell phone. She wasn't going to call him; she would just text him. It would give her a reason to text him. "I need oil dry and the good stuff, please. Time is moving so slowly here."

It didn't take him long to reply to her. "All I have is regular."

"I guess that will work. Couple bags please."

"K," was his only response.

It had been a while and he hadn't messaged her back, so she decided to send one more text. "Must be busy... I'm leaving when Dad gets back. Going to the store for some undergarments and a bottle of something yummy... I need a nap."

"Just steady.... Me, too." By the time he answered she was getting her stuff packed up to leave. She told her dad she was tired and explained what had happened the night before. She told him she was going to take a nap. She was so exhausted she felt as if she would throw up.

Cheyenne got back to the room and all of Sabrina's things were gone. She knew she would do this. So now she was stuck with a room and paying for it. She climbed up in the bed and covered up. The room was freezing. She knew it was also because she was tired. "You could come take a nap with me later... Boring here, I'm sitting here shivering. What is our topic for the day...?" She messaged to Sebastian.

"Tan lines." What kind of topic was that?

"Be more precise," she insisted. It wasn't long after she sent her message to Sebastian that she fell asleep.

11

When Cheyenne awoke, she realized she had slept almost 2 hours. It was almost 2 p.m. She needed to get up and run to the store because she had nothing to drink at the hotel. She rolled out of the bed, slipped into her shoes, and went to the closest gas station to get a few teas. Before leaving the gas station, she sent Sabastian a quick text. "Do you need anything before I go back to the room?"

It didn't take him long to respond: "No, I'm good, Baby."

She waited to send him anything else until she got back to the room. She started filling the tub for a bath so she could relax, but before she could climb into the tub, there was a knock at her door. "Just a minute," she hollered, slipping her shirt back on. She answered the door to find Sabrina standing in front of her. "Hey."

"Hey, I came back to hang with you for a while. Louis went to work," Sabrina said as she walked into the room.

"Well, I was getting into the tub."

"Ok, when you're done, we can run to the store and see if we can find any cute bras and undies."

"All right," Cheyenne said. She went into the bathroom and just wanted to sit in the tub and text Sebastian. She really had no desire to go to the store.

She sat down in the water, grabbed her phone from beside the tub, and fired off her first text to Sebastian. "Anyway... so, what about tan lines? Like, are we talking fake-bake or natural ones..."

His response was not how she had expected the conversation to go. "What's the best way to get rid of them?"

She looked at her phone for a while, unsure of what answer he was wanting from her. She thought about her answer before responding. "Is this like a trick question? Run around naked would be my guess." She finished her bath and got dressed. When she came out of the bathroom, Sabrina was standing by the door.

"Are you ready to go?" She asked Cheyenne.

"Yeah, how long have you been standing by the bathroom door?"

"Not too long, a few minutes. I figured you were about done."

They decided to take Sabrina's car. Cheyenne was over driving at this point, and she still felt a little off. "Soo... Darling..." she texted to Sebastian.

He replied within seconds. "Yes, dear?"

"Shopping is hard." She responded as she and Sabrina went into the store.

"Yes."

Cheyenne sent a picture of some red lingerie. It was a red-lace top with lace in the shape of hearts around the breasts. It had thin spaghetti straps with gold heart pieces, which sat nicely on each shoulder. The lingerie came with matching underwear. "Sabrina picked this out."

"Is that her making up outfit?" Sebastian asked.

Cheyenne giggled. "No, she told me to get them."

"Ohhhh," was all he replied.

"Do you approve?" she asked him. She thought she would get more of a response than she did.

"Yes, Ma'am," he replied, making her smile a little. She couldn't help but wonder if he was picturing her in the little outfit.

"Anything else I need? What about these tan lines, how do they disappear?" She asked him.

"Cut the area of your clothes out."

What kind of answer was that? It really seems like the same thing that she said. "Isn't that the same as running around naked?"

"I guess.... You have my permission," he replied.

She didn't know that she needed his permission to run around naked. They weren't together. Just then her phone started ringing. She looked down to see Automotive Parts Unlimited on the screen. "Hello?" She said, almost as a question and audible worry in her voice.

"Hey, Babe," came Sebastian's voice on the other end of the line.

"Is there something wrong?" Sebastian never called her from the work phone to her personal phone. If he did, normally something was wrong.

"Just wanted to talk to you. I had another one of my mini strokes that I have. Just feeling a little off now." Sebastian would have mini strokes, as he called them, where his speech wouldn't work. Afterwards he would be drained of energy. He said he would feel off the rest of the day. She had asked if he had seen a doctor for it, and he told her that he wasn't going to spend a lot of money to find out nothing.

He had them when he was stressed out. She knew that he was stressed about the new manager starting soon. Sebastian wanted the store, and they gave it to someone else.

"Oh, Honey. You want me to come over there? Do you need me to get you anything?" She asked him. She was worried about him.

"No, I don't need anything. Just called to talk a moment, but it's starting to get busy again. I'll talk to you when I get off work. Goodbye, Honey."

"Bye, Babe," she replied.

Since he didn't want her to go there, she decided to try on her new shirt and see what he thought. It was a gray tank top that said 'Good Vibes' on it. The gray on the shirt was a tie-died print with several different shades of gray. She sent him a picture of her wearing only the tank top. She added the words, "Does it look bad?"

Sebastian answered, "Looks fine."

"Ahh, my legs look fat in that picture." Now she wished she hadn't sent the picture, but it was too late now. She decided to change the subject. "Do I get 5 minutes of your time when you get off work?"

"Probably," he answered. She really wished that he would have given a yes or no answer instead of 'probably.'

"Are you ok to drive?" She asked him, since he still had to go let his dog out, she assumed.

"Yes, Ma'am."

"Room 205," was her next message to Sebastian. It had been about 20 minutes and she hadn't heard from him. She sent him another message. "You're slow, man."

"Just got done with work. Five phone calls after I left."

"So, are you coming here now?" She asked him. The longer he took, the more nervous she was becoming.

"Just leaving...... Got to go to Walgreens."

"I got your tea, just one. Tell me when here."

"Fucking pharmacy drive-thru." He messaged her.

"What do you need there?" She was pretty sure she didn't want to know the answer.

"Her pills," he replied.

"Oh." She didn't know what to say to him.

While she waited for him to get there, she picked up the room and set all the skittles that she didn't like on the entertainment center. It was a little while before she got another message from him. "I'm by the south door."

"Give me a minute to walk down."

~~~~

When they got back to the room, she kissed him a few times. Sebastian plopped down on his stomach on the bed. "I'm pretty sure I still owe you a massage. If you want it?" She asked.

"Not right now, Honey. I feel very tired after today," he said. Cheyenne tried not to let him see the disappointment on her face.

"Ok," she said.

She sat at the top of the bed. He moved quickly and rolled over onto her legs. Sebastian wiggled a little until he was between her legs. He was halfway sitting up but enough to be resting his head on her stomach and slightly on her chest. Cheyenne was barely on the bed and less on it now that he was on her. She bent her right knee and placed her foot on the bed to keep them both from falling off. Sebastian wrapped his arm around
~~~~

the leg she had bent, slowly ran his hand up in the leg of her pants, and lightly rubbed her bare leg.

Cheyenne rested her arms around his neck, placing her hands on his chest, one hand tucked down inside his shirt. Neither of them spoke a word. She didn't feel the need to say anything; she could tell he was comfortable lying there with her. There were other things she would really like to be doing with him, but this felt nice, too. She felt safe just being there in the room holding him.

She was sure that Sebastian fell asleep in her arms, but she really didn't mind, though. She enjoyed watching him. She just laid there propped up on her pillows, watching his chest rise and fall, wishing they had moments like this more often.

Cheyenne's phone played music in the background, and one of her favorite songs, *'Are you going to kiss me or not' by Thompson Square,* started to play. The song must have woken him, because as the chorus played, he started to tap Cheyenne's foot. She could hear him lightly singing the words. The only time he tapped her foot was during the same words of the song. She leaned down and kissed his forehead. He looked up and smiled at her his special smile.

Cheyenne was unsure how long they stayed there. She wanted the moment to last forever, but all good things must come to an end. "Honey, I better get going. I have a few things to do still," he said as he rolled over on her, bringing them face to face. She bent down and kissed his soft lips. He rubbed his body against her, as he slid his hand behind her neck.

His breathing quickened, turning his kisses harder. He suddenly stopped and pushed away. "I can't do this today."

"Did I do something wrong?" Cheyenne asked, trying not to cry.

"No," he said as he settled back down on top of her, this time using his arm to hold him slightly above her. "I just don't have much energy from earlier. Don't be mad, but I think I'm going to go home and take a nap."

As much as Cheyenne wanted him to stay with her, she understood. She was just happy that he came out to see her. "I'm not mad, I understand, Honey."

He leaned his head down to her and gave her another soft kiss on her lips. She couldn't believe how gentle he could be to her. Sebastian stood up between the two beds and pulled Cheyenne up to him, sliding one arm around her waist and cupping the back of her neck with the other. As he embraced her, he engaged her into another deep, passionate kiss...and then another.

"I really have to go," he said between the kisses.

This time Cheyenne pulled away. "Don't get me wrong, I don't want you to leave. But if you do not leave soon, I'm going to push you down on that bed and do things to you that I have wanted to do for a while. And as much as I want to do that, I know you don't feel well."

"Fair point," he said as she walked over to the entertainment center. She grabbed a purple Skittle. He picked up an orange one.

"Ewe you're going to eat an orange Skittle. That is the yucky kind," Cheyenne said as she wrinkled up her nose.

"Yes, I am. Don't you eat all of them?" Sebastian asked.

"No, I only like the red and purple ones." The rest taste funny.

Sebastian picked up a few of the yellow ones and ate them. He smiled when she wrinkled up her nose again. "Honey, you're a strange one."

"I know," was all she replied.

"Are you going to walk me down?" he asked her.

"Of course, I will," she answered.

They walked down the stairs, neither saying anything. He was popping more of the yellow Skittles in his mouth, smiling with each one. When they reached the door, he turned and pulled her into a hug. He kissed her with a deep, passionate kiss, before he pulled away. "You can text for a while before I go to bed."

"All right, I will." She leaned into him for one last kiss, and then he turned to walk out the door, and he was gone.

12

As the weeks went by, Sebastian and Cheyenne's love affair only intensified. She would stop by his work to see him every morning, and he would come down to see her at the shop almost every night. It was a Saturday morning when Sebastian called down to the shop and asked, "Can I come down and do my brakes today?"

"I'm not sure. The truck owned by the guy you sent down here the other day is still here. The one with the broken brake lines. Dad hasn't gotten it put back together yet, and I think he is having issues with it," Cheyenne said.

"Do you want me to come down and help?" He asked.

"That's up to you. If you want."

"I'll be down in a minute," Sebastian said. "Is the door unlocked?"

"No, I'll sit in the office and wait for you so I can let you in." Cheyenne said, trying to hold in her excitement. She was going to see him today. When he pulled up to the shop, her heart started to race. She met him at the door and unlocked it and then relocked it once he was inside. Before he could walk away from her, she pushed him against the wall and kissed him. It wasn't a very long kiss, but it was more than enough to get her excited – and moderately wet.

Sebastian returned the kiss but then quickly pushed her away. "Your dad is around the corner." He pulled her in and kissed her one more time. "So no more," he asserted, breathing heavily through his words.

"Fine," She pouted. "I'll go back to the office then." She smiled as she strolled slowly towards the office. When she turned back to cast a glance at him, he was still standing against the wall, watching her. He looked amazing. She was unsure why he was still wearing his black work clothes.

As she entered the shop, she found her dad sitting by his toolbox, watching his tablet. "Hey, Timmy," Sebastian said. Cheyenne's dad hated to be called Timmy. There were only a few people who could get away with it. Sebastian happened to be one of them. "I was going to see if I could work on my brakes today, but I see you still have that truck here. Do you want some help getting the brake lines done?" Sebastian asked.

"Sure," Cheyenne's dad replied.

Her dad climbed under the truck, and he and Sebastian spoke about what they could do to fix it. Cheyenne would hand them the tools as they needed them. She was leaning over the motor to grab the brake line to pull it up to the master cylinder when Sebastian grabbed her ass. She let out a small scream, as he startled her. The more she bent over the motor, the more you could see her purple lace thong underwear. She bent over further, now that she knew he was watching her.

Sebastian showed her a photo on his phone. The image was of exotic dancers decorated in paint that reacted to black light. She picked up her phone and texted him so her dad wouldn't hear her. "Is that a strip club?"

"Yup," was his reply.

"Neat! Is that here in Iowa?"

"Ames," he said.

They worked on the brake lines until they needed parts. They needed smaller wrenches, but Cheyenne's dad didn't have any small enough, so Sebastian ran to his house to get one." I'll text you when I get back so you can let me in," he said at the door as he gave her a small peck on the lips.

"Ok," she said as she locked the door behind him.

After he left, she sent him another message. "You suck."

His reply was simple. "Sure." Cheyenne rolled her eyes at his answer.

"I hate that word, you know. All questions have some sort of yes or no answers." She messaged him back.

Once again, he replied with, "sure."

This time she just let it go. She only replied with "dick."

"I'm back," he replied.

"K." She walked up to the door to unlock it. He walked past her, slightly rubbing her vagina. Cheyenne grabbed him by the hand and pulled him back to her. Their eyes locked and, for a brief moment, it was just him and her, seemingly alone in the world. He pulled her into a kiss, as he slid one hand down the front of her pants.

When his hands met their goal, she let out a moan of satisfaction. She was unsure what turned her on more, the idea that her dad could come right around the corner and see them, or what his hands were doing to her. She went to untuck his shirt when he stopped her. "No. We can't right now." He pulled away and smiled. He took the wrenches back to her dad. She had to stand there for a moment to regain control of herself. She was absolutely tingling, and all of her senses were aroused. Her lacy thong now felt warm and creamy beneath her jeans.

When she walked back to the shop her dad asked, "What is the thermostat at?"

"It's at 69, where I set it. I was cold," she said with a smile. A few minutes later her phone went off in her pocket. She had it on vibrate so no one would know she was texting.

The message was from Sebastian. "So, 69 is your 'Comfort level?'" She smiled and looked up at him after she read it.

"Maybe... Maybe not... Grrr," she replied to him.

"Don't make me eat you," he wrote while standing right next to her. She could smell his sweet scent. He was driving her crazy by using every opportunity to brush against her, tease her. She was starting to lose her composure.

"Really now, you're all talk... Just saying." She added a kissy face emoji at the end of the message. Then she waited a minute and wrote, "Don't make threats you can't keep."

"We need some compression fittings. Cheyenne, can you run and get some?" Cheyenne's dad asked her.

Sebastian handed her some money. "Go down the road to O'Reilly and get a ¼ compression fitting. Get a few if you can, just in case we need them."

Cheyenne went down to get the fittings and then had to come back; Sebastian didn't give her enough money, and she had forgotten her wallet. She could have just run to the other parts store, one that would let her charge, but she needed more time to cool down. Just looking at Sebastian was driving her wild. She wanted to touch him so badly. She was beginning to not care about what her dad thought anymore.

She walked back to the shop and said, "I've got to run back down to the parts store. I didn't have enough cash on me, and I had to return to get my wallet."

"Why didn't you just go to my store?" Sebastian asked with a little bit of attitude.

"Well... I didn't think of that," she replied.

Cheyenne turned around and left. Before she even got to the car, she received a text from Sebastian. "Sorry.... Didn't mean to be a dick."

"Huh?" She then realized he was talking about his attitude a minute ago. "I needed extra time to calm down... Soooo yep."

"About?" He replied.

"Well, IDK, think about it. I'm not mad, just idk. You still suck, FYI."

"Sure," he replied. Then he said, "Think about what?"

Cheyenne took a deep breath before she replied to him again. "Why would I need to calm down? HMM IDK maybe you are driving me crazy! I'm about to do things that would... well...dude that word is going to get you spanked."

When Cheyenne returned, he smiled when he watched her walk over to him. They finished up the brake lines on the truck. Her dad took it out for a drive to make sure the breaks worked properly.

When her dad left with the truck, Cheyenne shut the garage door behind him. Sebastian walked up behind her, wrapped his arms around her, and bent down and started to kiss her neck, nibbling slightly. She leaned back into his body and into his kisses. With every kiss she tipped her head more and more to the side. He was making it gooshy between her legs - again. As he kissed her, he slid one of his hands down her pants, slowly twirling her hair, and then sliding a finger inside of her.

"Oh my God," she moaned. "Stop," she begged. She reached back and rubbed his hard cock.

Sebastian's only response was, "See? The neck is sensational." He leaned around and kissed her lips. They both saw the headlights in front of the window. They looked at each other and pulled themselves apart. "Unlock your phone and turn your camera on."

She didn't answer him. She just did as she was directed. Sebastian went to the bathroom while Cheyenne went to unlock the front door for her dad. As Sebastian walked out of the bathroom, he nonchalantly slid her phone in her hand. She had a message from him on the phone already. It said, "Check your photos."

She ignored the message and slid the phone back in her pocket of her jeans. She was pretty sure she knew what photo he was talking about. He owed her a photo. He promised to send her one a while ago, but he always chickened out. Sebastian and her dad talked while waiting for the other guy to pick up his truck. After he came, they all said their goodbyes and left.

13

"What do you mean she threw him out?" Grace asked with a slight raise to her voice. Grace was Marie's stepdaughter. Grace was 14, but she much older. She was almost as tall as Cheyenne, with dark-red hair and blue eyes. She was a beautiful girl. Cheyenne's dad nicknamed her Squeaky, so that is what everyone called her.

"That is what he said when he just called from his work phone," Cheyenne said. She also turned his phone off. Sebastian told me he was going to get a new phone and would call me back later. He was complaining that he got lost because he couldn't use his GPS since he had no cell service."

"What was her reasoning for turning off the phone and kicking him out? Did she find out about you two?" Marie asked. Marie was short, about 5-foot-4. She was a small, skinny thing, but she had a mouth to hold her ground. She had brown eyes and curly, black hair, which hit about her shoulders.

"He told me she did it because he had gone to lunch with a female friend of his. I don't think she found out about us. He didn't say anything to me about that, just that he had gone to lunch with a friend he has known since he was a kid. I guess she posted a picture of them together on Facebook. Like I said, I don't know everything. We only talked for a few minutes," Cheyenne said. "He said he was mainly calling to let me know he was safe and back in Iowa.

A few minutes later, her phone rang again. She looked down to see Automotive Parts Unlimited on the caller ID. "Hello?"

"Hey, so I got my other phone. I'm trying to figure it out. It says I need the Internet to set it up. Then I'm going somewhere to get drunk," Sebastian said over the phone.

"Why?" She asked him.

"Because I have had a shitty day. I am completely over it."

"Why don't you come up to Marie's and hang out with us?" Cheyenne asked. "I'm staying here tonight; you could stay too. Or do you have somewhere else you plan on staying?"

"Is it ok with your friend if I come up there?" He asked.

"I'm sure it is. I already told her I wanted to hang out with you, and she was fine with that."

"If you're sure I can, I will come up there. I will call you when I am on my way there. Could you do me a favor and go get me a pack of smokes and something to drink?"

"Do you want some tea or beer?" Cheyenne asked.

"Beer, please. Thank you," he said.

"Ok, talk to you soon. Bye." Cheyenne hung up andwent and told Marie that he was coming up to the house. Marie seemed excited to meet him. She had briefly met him once before, but it was at his work and only for a few minutes. Cheyenne decided to run up to corner convenience store to get what he asked her to pick up. She was leaving the store when her phone rang. She didn't know the number, but she thought that it might be Sebastian, so she answered it with a question in her voice. "Hello?"

"Hey, babe. I'm on my way there. Do you want to meet me at the tire place in town? Then I'll just follow you to her house." Sebastian asked.

"Yeah, I can. How long until you get there?"

"Wait like 10 minutes and then leave."

"Ok," Cheyenne said, trying not to sound too excited. She was finally going to get to see him. It had been over a week since she had seen him last. Cheyenne decided to just head to the tire place, but she was unsure where it was. She asked Grace to go along and show her how to get there.

They drove to the place just off Main Street. She had no idea how she had never noticed the place before. She pulled in and parked her car while they waited for Sebastian. When they saw his car approaching, she started the car and backed out. He stopped in the road and waited for her to go first. Cheyenne drove back to Marie's and parked her loaner car in front of the house. Sebastian parked beside her.

As she glanced out the car window, he looked over and smiled at her. She melted right there. Cheyenne walked over to him and threw her arms around his neck, taking in his sweet scent. She lightly kissed his neck. "I've missed you." She hugged him tightly. She didn't want to let him go.

"I've missed you, too," he said as he wrapped his arms around her waist. He slightly pushed her away from him and looked her up and down. Before he could do anything, she put her lips to his. He wrapped his arm around the small of her back, pulling her in for a more intense kiss.

Cheyenne let out a small moan underneath his kisses. "Honey, as much as I want to stay here in your arms forever, we should probably go out back with everyone. They have been wanting to meet you."

"Yeah, you're probably right. Lead the way," Sebastian said as he lightly slapped her on the bottom. They went through the house to the back porch but stopped in the kitchen to grab him a shot of peach Crown and a couple beers to take outside. She grabbed herself a Twisted Tea. Out back was Marie, her boyfriend, Terry, his brother Paul, and Grace. Paul was slightly shorter than Cheyenne, with brown hair and brown eyes. He was already three sheets to the wind. Terry, who was taller than Paul, kept his head shaved and was very muscular. He was the only adult who wasn't drinking.

Cheyenne introduced everyone to Sebastian. As Sebastian walked down the steps of the deck Paul spoke up first. "Is that your dad?" Cheyenne covered her face. She was so embarrassed. Cheyenne was unsure if Sebastian heard what Paul said about him. If he did, he just ignored the remark.

"No, Paul, that is not her dad. Just shut up." Terry snipped at Paul.

After talking and having a good time for a while, Paul asked, "Sebastian, are you and Cheyenne together?"

"No!" Cheyenne and Sebastian answered at the same time. She wanted to answer differently, but she knew deep down she was nothing more than a fling, even if she didn't want to admit it to herself. Everything was going well. They were all talking and picking songs that they all loved to hear. Sebastian and Grace seemed to like a lot of the same songs.

"Hey, Grace, have you heard of *Blue October*?" Sebastian asked.

"Yeah, Cheyenne has a few songs on her phone's playlist by them." She started to play *'Hate Me'*.

"Cool," he said. "This is a good song. You should play '*The Worry List.*'"

Suddenly Paul said, "Cheyenne, you can sit on my lap. I could do so much to you. And, if you touch me, you'll fall in love with me. Come give me a hug."

"Paul, I'm not going to hug you. Nor will I fall in love with you." Little did he know she already had her love with her. Before she could get up off the bench she was sitting on, Sebastian was already in Paul's face.

"You want to fight an old man?" Sebastian asked Paul.

"I'll fight you," Paul said as he stood up. He was about half a foot shorter than Sebastian.

"Knock it off, you two." Terry defused the situation by getting between the two. "Cheyenne, please take Sebastian out front to cool off."

Cheyenne grabbed Sebastian by the hand and started to pull him away from Paul. "Come with me, Sebastian. We can take a little walk." Sebastian started to walk away with Cheyenne when Paul yelled at him.

"Oh, you have to have girls protect you, old man." Paul yelled from behind Terry.

Sebastian dropped Cheyenne's hand and started to turn back around. When he turned halfway around, Grace was there to stop him. "Come on, Sebastian, let's go with Cheyenne." Grace spoke with a calm tone, even though you could tell she was angry.

"Fine," Sebastian muttered under his breath. Cheyenne, Grace and Sebastian went out front. "Just leave me alone for a minute," Sebastian barked at the girls. Both of them went inside the house. Cheyenne grabbed a tea and got him another beer. She waited for a few minutes before she went back outside.

Sebastian was standing by the large Cedar tree in the front yard. She walked up to him and wrapped her arms around his waist and laid her head on his chest. He returned the gesture. He wrapped his arms around her and rested his chin on her head. "What's the matter, Babe?" She asked him in a soft voice.

"He's being a dick to the kids." Cheyenne hadn't seen Paul be mean to anyone besides running his mouth to her.

"Oh, well... I don't know. I didn't see him being mean to anyone. I'm sure Terry has him calmed down. Do you want to go back with everyone?" She asked. "I brought you a beer."

"Thanks, Honey. Can we just stand her for a minute?" He took the beer and bent down and kissed her lips.

"Yeah, we can," she whispered between his kisses. Sebastian backed her against the tree. He reached down and wrapped his arms around her thighs just below her buttocks. Grabbing her with a firm grip, he stood back up, picking her up with him. Cheyenne wrapped her legs around him. His hand slid up her shirt, just as his lips met hers. She felt her back against the rough tree bark, but she didn't care.

Cheyenne heard someone walking up behind them. "I think someone is coming," Sebastian said.

"Cheyenne, it's Grace. Marie asked if you guys are coming back."

"Yeah, we can go back," Sebastian said. Cheyenne figured that Sebastian would put her down, but he didn't. He continued to kiss her neck.

"Talk about a buzz-kill," Cheyenne whispered. "Grace, we will be right there," she added in a louder tone.

"I think she is ruining our fun," Sebastian whispered.

"I think you're right," she giggled.

"You guys know I can still hear you, right?" Grace added from the other side of the tree.

"We will be there in a minute," Sebastian growled as he continued to hold Cheyenne up against the tree. "You know we could just continue and not go back to the party," Sebastian added as he heard Grace walk away.

"We could, but Marie will be mad at us if we don't go back."

"You are probably right. Let's go back," Sebastian said as he lowered

Cheyenne to the ground. He kissed her a few more times before he picked his beer up off the ground. Hand in hand they walked back towards their friends.

~~~~

Sebastian walked up to Paul. "Hey man, I was wrong, and I shouldn't have gotten in your face."

"It's all right," Paul said as they both 'bro-hugged.' Cheyenne thought they were going to hug forever. She started to get a little jealous.

The group of friends went back to having a great time until Paul smarted off something else to Cheyenne. "You can ride me if you want?"

"Shut up, Paul," Marie yelled. "You just need to go home."

Paul just laughed. Whenever he would get drunk, he would think that everyone wanted to be with him, and he would laugh for no reason at all. Marie hated having Paul there when he was drinking.

When Sebastian heard what he said, he started for the porch where Paul was sitting. Marie stood in front of the stairs. Cheyenne walked up behind Sebastian and wrapped her arms around him." Please, don't, Sebastian.

"He can't say that shit. I am either going to beat the shit out of him, or I'm leaving." Sebastian said angrily.

"Where are you going?" Cheyenne asked.

"To a hotel," Sebastian spitted out. Cheyenne, who still had her arms around him, slipped her hand in his pocket and took out his key. Holding it tightly in her hand, she was hoping he wouldn't notice she had pick-pocketed him. She thought he was probably too drunk to notice he no longer had his key.

"Will you let me drive you? I have had less to drink than you." Cheyenne paused. "Please," she begged him as she slid her hand into his.

"Fine," he replied. She could tell he was angry. He was shaking. She had never seen him angry like this before.

It didn't take long for them to say goodbye to everyone. Neither of them said anything to Paul. In her opinion Paul had ruined the fun they were having. He always acted like a child when he drank.

~~~~

Cheyenne sat behind the wheel of her loaner car. She fastened her seatbelt and looked over to the passenger seat to be sure Sebastian was buckled in, too. Her loaner car was a silver Nissan. She acquired it after she hit a deer, wrecking her Jeep. She was ready to have her Jeep back. This was a very nice car, but it wasn't her Jeep.

“Are you ready to go?" Cheyenne asked.

“Yeah, I'm ready. Are we going to a hotel?" Sebastian asked.

“Yes, we will go to Marshalltown and see if we can find one,” she said as she backed out of the driveway. She was nervous about driving. She had, had a few drinks; more than a few in fact. They had been drinking since about 4 p.m. As they drove towards the outskirts of the town, Cheyenne looked over and saw that Sebastian was passed out in the seat beside her.

When she approached the corner where she needed to turn, she came to a stop. Sebastian started to stir. He sat up in his seat as she turned. “Where are you going? This is not the right way,” he said as she turned left.

“Yes, it is. Just lay back and relax,” Cheyenne said as she rested her hand on his hand. He placed her hand in his. He started to lay back in the seat again and then drifted off to sleep.

She drove to town making sure to drive the speed limit. As she slowly headed towards the hotels, she was thankful she hadn't seen any cars or people. She pulled into the Comfort Inn and walked inside to see if they had any available rooms. She drove to three more hotels, but none of them had a vacancy. As she was pulling away from the last one, Sebastian woke up. “Do they have any rooms?”

“No, so far no one has any rooms available,” she replied.

“Which ones have you gone to?” He asked.

“Comfort Inn, Best Western, Super 8, and Hampton Inn are the ones I have tried. Do you know of any others you would like to try?”

“There is a crappy one down that way,” he said as he pointed to the west. “It is called the Budget Inn. It is not a very nice one, but it will work,” Sebastian said.

“Honey, I don't think it is open,” Cheyenne said as they pulled in.

She pulled up to the door and Sebastian got out of the car. He walked up to the office door. The building was a tan color, or maybe it was just dirt. It appeared to be rundown. The place gave her a bad feeling. The office door was locked, and for some reason, she let out a sigh of relief.

Sebastian got back in the car. "They must be full, otherwise the door is normally open. Let's try the one by Wendy's."

She just nodded and pulled out to the highway again. She turned down a few roads and pulled into the Motel 6. "You are going in this time. I'm getting tired," Cheyenne said.

Without saying anything, he just got out of the car and headed inside. A moment later he opened the door and yelled out to her. "Honey, can you come here? They need your phone number. I don't have one to use."

She rolled her eyes at him. He just didn't know his new number. She got out of the car and went to the door as he held it open for her. "They have a room," he added.

Cheyenne walked up to the front desk with Sebastian right beside her. When she approached the desk, Sebastian's license was sitting on the counter. She picked it up and looked at it before she handed it to him. "I'll put it in my name." She grabbed her wallet and took out her information and her credit card.

"Thank you!" Sebastian said as he put his arm around her waist. She knew he didn't want anyone to know where he was. He was afraid that Sarah would come and take his car from him.

She thanked the man at the desk when he gave them their room number and keys. The man gave them directions to their room. Sebastian and Cheyenne walked back out to the car to drive it around the building and park near their room.

Cheyenne went too far and went over the edge of the parking spot a bit. "Back in, Honey." Sebastian said.

"I cannot back up very well." She backed the car up again and tried to position it better. Over the edge she went again with the one tire. She put the car in reverse one last time, backed up and was about to try again when Sebastian spoke.

"Honey, you head upstairs to the room; I'll back the car in the parking spot. I'll be up after I finish smoking." He leaned over and gave her a kiss on her cheek. Cheyenne put the car in park.

"Ok. I'll wait for you upstairs in the room," she said as she got out of the car and started to walk towards the hotel. She turned around before she went through the door and saw that he already had the car turned around and backed into the parking space. Cheyenne rolled her eyes, even though she knew he couldn't see it.

She headed up to the room, unlocked the door, and flipped on the light. The room was not a very nice room, but it wasn't horrible. Just inside the room and to the left was the bathroom. Straight in from the door was a desk, against which was a mini fridge. Hanging on the wall above it was a TV. In front of the desk were two beds, and between those sat a small table with two lamps. One of the beds had cigarette burns on the orange-colored bedspread.

Cheyenne picked the bed with no holes and stole one of the pillows off the other bed. She pulled the sheets down, slipped off her sandals, and crawled into bed. She pulled the blanket up over her, but as soon as she got comfortable, she decided it needed to be warmer in the room, so she got up and ran over to turn on the heat. She knew that Sebastian was going to lecture her about making it too hot in the room. She ran back over to the bed and crawled beneath the covers. She wasn't there long before Sebastian entered.

"Wow, it's hot in here," Sebastian said as he feigned to be dying of a heat stroke.

"It is nice. I was cold."

"Well... Honey, we're going to have to turn the air on or the heat off," he said.

"Fine, turn on the air." He walked over and turned on the air-conditioner. He walked to the bathroom and came back shortly after. As he walked over to the beds, he glanced over at the one with burn holes. "That bed looks a little rough. I bet I'll get that bed."

Cheyenne smiled. "Yep, I got the nicer one."

"Yup, I'm thinking I'm sleeping over there," he said as he pointed to the other side of Cheyenne's bed.

"If you want to," she said with a playful smile. "Or you can sleep over there by yourself. Up to you," she said as she shrugged her shoulders. Cheyenne was trying to act like it didn't matter to her where he slept, but in actuality, it did. She slipped off her shirt so she could remove her bra and then grabbed her shirt and pulled it back over her head. She looked up at Sebastian, who was staring at her. "Yes, Dear?"

"Are you going to sleep with your clothes on?" He asked, kicking off his shoes and pulling down his pants to reveal his black Hanes boxers.

"I don't know, maybe," Cheyenne said as she tried to look only into his eyes and not at his body.

"Do you always sleep with clothes on?" He asked as he pulled his black shirt over his head.

"Yeah, don't you?"

"No, I always sleep naked." He paused and pulled his boxers down to his feet and slowly stepped out of them. She could see that he was fully erect. "Let me help you undress, Love." He walked over to the bed and pulled her black T-shirt over her head.He flung her shirt over his head, and it landed on the floor behind him. Cheyenne was unsure where it ended up, and she really didn't care. He reached down with his right hand and started caressing her left breast. He slowly knelt and pushed her onto the bed. Sebastian climbed on her, nibbling on her nipples until a colossal moan escape her lips.

14

He tugged at her shorts, pulling them down around her ankles and sliding them off over her feet. "Aww, no underwear, Honey... Mmm," he said as he bent down and kissed her inner thigh.

Cheyenne started to squirm as his lips touched her thigh. She felt a shiver move down her spine, and her body tingled with anticipation of what was to come. He put his finger slightly inside her. "MMM, you're teasing. That's not very nice," she said, moving towards his fingers. The closer she moved towards them, the further he pulled away from her.

"Seems someone is a bit eager," Sebastian said as he pulled her up to a standing position. He cupped the back of her neck with his left hand and placed his right hand at the back of her waist, finally letting it rest on the small of her back and pulled her in close to him. Sebastian bent down to kiss her, slowly at first, but soon his kisses were deep and intense. The force he used hurt her mouth, but at the same time it drove her wild with sexual desire.

Cheyenne decided it was her turn to take control. She pulled away from his firm grasp and intoxicating kisses. He tried to pull her back, but she put her hands between them and pushed him down on the other bed.

"My turn to play." Cheyenne knelt between his legs. She thought about teasing him for a moment but decided against it. She grabbed the shaft of his large, hard cock and bent closer, lowering her tongue to him. She started at the area where his balls and penis connected and slowly raised one hand up to lightly massage his balls while swirling her tongue around the entire circumference, making her way up his shaft. When she reached the top, she licked between the slit on the tip, as she opened her mouth. Cheyenne nibbled the tip as she twirled her tongue around the head multiple times. She could feel him growing harder, as she slid the whole tip in her mouth, closing it around the entire shaft. She shoved it down her throat as far as she could while running one hand up and down the length of it and swirling her tongue.

Cheyenne sucked as she flattened her tongue to slide it up and down his shaft. Sebastian let out a whimper. He grabbed her hair. "Stop! Stop! If you don't, I'm going to cum." When she ignored his pleads, he yanked her hair tighter and jerked her head up to look at him. She stopped and gave him the best smile she could do with his cock still stationed in her mouth. When their eyes locked, Sebastian spoke again. "Please; stop for a moment. Where is your phone?"

She stood for a moment and looked around. When she found the phone, she handed it to him. "Why do you want my phone?" She asked, even though she was pretty sure why he wanted it.

"Unlock it for me and turn on the camera," he said as he handed the phone back to her. Cheyenne entered the code and did as he directed her. The thought of him taking pictures or recording them together was turning her on even more. He laid back on the bed. "You may continue." He said as he started to record her.

Cheyenne resumed her little oral sex act by getting on her knees, grabbing his cock in her hand and rubbing the tip with her fingers. She looked up into his eyes as she shoved the hole shaft in her mouth. Her eyes met his again, and while their eyes were locked, she shoved the whole shaft in her mouth. She sucked and teased, determined to make him beg for more.

Sebastian wiped the hair out of Cheyenne's face. He held her hair up and watched her suck on the tip of his cock. "Suck, Baby. Faster. Suck it like you want me to fuck you," he growled.

"What?" She asked as she stopped and looked at him. She had been lost in what she was doing and did not hear what he said the first time.

"Suck it like you want me to fuck you!" He said in a deep voice.

"Maybe I just want to tease you." She took the phone from him and threw it on the bed. She went to climb on top of him, but he was faster than her, and he stood up. He pushed her hard, and she landed on the other bed. His force towards her was so much different than the last time they were together. She thought it was very hot, and she loved it. Cheyenne was always in control when she was with someone. She had never been the submissive one in bed. This was all new to her, and she was very turned on by it.

"My turn, Honey," he said as he picked her up and set her more up on the bed. Sebastian lifted her legs up and climbed on top of her. Her legs rested firmly in the muscles of his arms. He gripped her legs and pulled her closer to him. When she was close enough, he slammed his cock into her. It caught her off guard and she let out a small whimper. He moved slowly coming out of her but every time he went inside, he would slam himself in her with a deep, hard thrust. Every thrust was harder and harder. He dropped her legs and slid them under his. Cheyenne was on the brink of exploding. He laid on top of her and cupped her left breast in his hand as he started to move again. His moans were getting intensely louder and louder with every movement. The sound of him alone was getting Cheyenne off. She had never heard a man enjoy himself so much while being inside her. With one last hard thrust in her, she let go of herself. She let herself explode around his hard cock. He must have felt her intense orgasm because he exploded inside of her.

Sebastian collapsed on top of her. "That was amazing," she whispered. She rubbed her fingertips along his back.

"Yes," was all he said in a low voice. He rolled off her, sliding his arm underneath her, bringing her closer to him. He laid on his back and she snuggled up to him, resting her head on his chest. He pulled the blanket up around them both. It didn't take long before she was fast asleep beside him.

The next thing she knew, Sebastian was above her, between her legs. She could barely see him in the dark, but she could feel his hands rubbing her legs. "You ready?" He asked as he slid two fingers inside of her.

He laid down on the bed between her legs and slowly licked her clit. Cheyenne moaned and squirmed. He sucked, licked and worked his magic on her. All her senses were aroused. "Oh, my God!" She exclaimed.

"You want to try something?" He asked.

Cheyenne looked at him with a pleading look. She would do anything he asked of her in the bedroom. The feelings, orgasms, the rush that she got for being with him, it was nothing like she had ever felt before. She nodded as she said, "Yes."

Sebastian pulled her up off the bed. "Bend over." She knelt on the bed, sticking her ass in his direction. She braced herself on the bed with her hands, gripping the bedsheet and blanket. Sticking his hands slightly inside her, he rubbed her clit, getting her wetter. Then he bent down and gave her a small lick before sticking his tongue deep inside her. He twirled his tongue around inside her before pulling it back out. "Mmm, don't you taste good," he said as he licked her clit one last time.

"Please, I want you inside me," Cheyenne begged. He stuck the head of his cock into her vagina and grabbed her thighs with each hand to give himself some leverage, and slowly eased himself inside her. She could feel his cock throbbing with every movement, and she could feel her body building up to a climactic explosion. As he moved, she moved with him. Each movement was in sync with the other. He slid one hand up her back, then up to her hair, lightly pulling it back into his fist. As he slammed himself in her, he tightened the grip on her hair. Then with one last thrust, he exploded inside of her. He fell over on top of her, which caused them both to fall onto the bed.

He rolled off her so she could roll over to face him. "Are you going to let me sleep now?" She asked playfully as she ran her hand up and down his chest.

"Ehh, sleep is overrated. You don't need any sleep," he said as he kissed her gently on her lips. His kisses moved from gentle to forceful, and Cheyenne started to gasp between the kisses.

"It's 4 in the morning; we need to get some sleep," Cheyenne said as best she could between his kisses. He didn't stop kissing her. Rather, he grabbed her hand with his and put her hand between her own legs.

"I'm going to go to the bathroom," he said. "And while I'm gone, I want you to continue to play with yourself." He reached over and flipped on the light. "I mean it. Sebastian stood up and started to walk towards the bathroom and then stopped and turned back towards her. "When I come back out, you had better still be playing." This time he gave her a stern look, his hands resting on his naked hips. The way he looked made Cheyenne giggle.

He walked off towards the bathroom, and Cheyenne stared at his body as he walked away. She could stare at Sebastian all day long; she was never bored of looking at him. When she saw the light turned off, she continued to massage herself. He has a point on the situation; he told her one day, *if you do it yourself, you can do what you like*. It did feel good. She figured out the places she liked to be touched and what she didn't like. She closed her eyes as she touched and rubbed herself. She felt other hands between her legs.

"Keep your eyes closed." She did as she was told. She felt his hands lightly touching her stomach, his finger swirling around her light-purple rose belly ring. Then she felt his tongue lightly touch it. His lips touched below her belly button. His kisses felt like phantom kisses, barely touching the skin, yet enough for her to feel. He kissed his way down her stomach.

"Please!" She begged. She felt him climb on top of her. Cheyenne couldn't keep her eyes closed any longer. He was smiling on top of her. "What?" She asked.

"Nothing," he said. She didn't believe that he had nothing to say, but she didn't want to fight with him, so she just let it go. She smiled back at him and then leaned up to kiss his soft lips. She rubbed his cheek, feeling his 5 o'clock shadow. Cheyenne couldn't believe that she was in bed with this man. The way he made her feel was amazing – free and loved. "What are you thinking about?" He asked her.

"Nothing, really," she said. "I just wish this night would never end."

"Aww, Honey, I wish I could stop time, but I can't. We can just live for the moment." He lowered his mouth to hers, slipping his tongue in slightly. He acted as if it was the first time they had kissed; exploring her kisses, running his hands down her body. She started to moan with the way his hands felt on her, so soft and so gentle. "You want me to stop?"

"No," she whispered. She pulled his head down to her so that she could reach his neck. She kissed it gently. He moaned the more she kissed. She felt him slide inside her.

This time he was slow and gentle. He caressed her breasts as he moved. He kissed her lips with a slight nibble, and then moved to her cheek, her ear, and then down her neck. His movements stayed steady. Cheyenne lifted her legs and wrapped them around him. This must have turned Sebastian on because he started to move faster. He no longer kissed her; he slid his hands under her shoulders, gripping the top of her shoulders with his fingers. He used his hands to hold her in place as he thrusted hard. This time he didn't wait for her to get her release, but she didn't care; she was too wrapped up in the moment. When he exploded, he slammed himself so far up in her she let out a small scream.

He rolled off her and laid on his back for a moment before he turned over on his side facing her. "Thank you," he said as he wrapped his arm around her. He snuggled his head into her shoulder and was asleep within minutes. She laid there watching him sleep for a while before she reached over and flipped off the light. She rested her free hand on his. He took his hand out from hers and put his on top and gripped her hand tightly. She was unsure if he woke up for a moment or if he grabbed her hand in his sleep. She really didn't care. She was just glad to be in his arms. She felt safe in his arms – and loved.

15

Cheyenne woke up and rolled over to check the time on her phone. It was only 7:30 in the morning. *Why was she awake at this time?* Then she remembered where she was and who she was with. She couldn't believe he stayed all night with her, just like she had wanted for so long. Once she had asked him to tell his girlfriend that he was leaving for a weekend and just stay with her somewhere. She wanted to show him they could stay together and be ok. And he finally stayed all night. She rolled back over and gave him a small kiss on the cheek. He let out a small moan, which made her smile.

When Cheyenne stood up to head to the bathroom, her head started to spin. Her body hurt all over. She wasn't sure if it was from the active night, the alcohol, or the lack of sleep.

When she came back to bed Sebastian was still asleep. She cuddled up beside him as he slept on his side, facing away from her. "Sebastian, wake up." Then he mumbled and started to stir.

"Huh?" He rolled on his back. "Yes, I'm awake." His eyes were still closed. She knew he wasn't awake. He peeked out of one eye, the one closest to her, and smiled.

"I'm going to run to the gas station to get something to drink and something for my head. Do you want anything?"

"Tea, please," he said as he started to snore again.

Cheyenne giggled at him. "Anything else?"

He mumbled again before saying, "Something to feed the monkeys."

"Monkeys?" She asked in a full laughter. Cheyenne gave him a small peck on his cheek. He didn't respond to her, so she got up, found her clothes, slipped them on, and grabbed the room key. Then she sneaked out the door, being extra careful not to wake him.

She drove down the road to the gas station and grabbed a few teas. She knew he liked sweet tea. When she got back to the hotel, she remembered that she had forgotten the ibuprofen. She got her phone out and called Jennie, hoping she would have some she could drop off on her way to work.

"What do you want, woman?" Jennie said when she answered the phone.

"To tell you I love you... and can you bring me some ibuprofen before I blow chunks all over the place?" Cheyenne asked in the sweetest tone she could manage.

"Where are you?" She asked.

"At the hotel by Wendy's. I can wait for you on the backside of the building."

"Who's with you?" Jennie asked.

"Outside, just me." Cheyenne answered. "Inside, Sebastian."

"Is he going to be outside with you?"

"No, he's sleeping. I wasn't going to wake him up."

"Ok, give me a minute to get dressed for work and then I'll be over."

"Thank you. See ya in a bit," Cheyenne said. She was glad that Jennie answered this early. Her head was killing her.

"K, bye," Jennie replied in a smart-ass tone. Some days she wondered why she and Jennie were best friends because there were days that Cheyenne wanted to choke her because of her mouth. Jennie didn't even let her say goodbye before she hung up, which was nothing new. Jennie, Marie and Cheyenne had been best friends for years. Grace was Marie's step-daughter, but they consider her just one of the girls.

Cheyenne was starting to regret the shots she took last night, but she was really proud of herself for keeping up with Sebastian. She was normally a lightweight, but last night she held her own. It wasn't long before Jennie was calling.

"Hello," Cheyenne answered.

"Where are you? I'm by the side of the building," Jennie said.

"I am sitting outside by the door. Go to the other door," Cheyenne said.

Within a few minutes Jennie pulled around to where she was sitting and pulled up beside her. Cheyenne got up and walked over to the tan Chevy Equinox and climbed into the passenger seat. Jennie didn't even wait for the door to shut before she spoke.

"What are you doing here, and why are you with Sebastian?" She asked as she raised an eyebrow at her.

"Well, last night we were at a party, and he and another guy kept getting into it. Sebastian was telling everyone that it was because the other guy was being mean to the kids. I'm not sure of his real reasoning. Well, it got to the point that they were going to fight. Sebastian was going to drive himself to a hotel. He drank more than me, so, I offered to drive him to a hotel. It took us a few tries to find one that had a room available. This was the last hotel left in town. He wanted me to stay with him, so I did. And let me tell you it was amazing! This might be the best 24 hours I've had in a long time," Cheyenne said with a sheepish grin.

"I see. I'm glad you're having fun," Jennie said, glancing down at the time. "I have to get to work. I'll call you when I get off," she said as she handed her the bottle of Ibuprofen. "Take as many as you want." Cheyenne took the bottle and took out eight of the pills. She wanted to make sure she had enough for both her and Sebastian.

"Thank you. I'll talk to you after work." Cheyenne got out of the car and headed back inside. She trudged up the stairs, pretty sure he was still sleeping. She wanted to go back to sleep, but she knew that was not going to happen. She stood in front of the door to the room for a while. She wanted to go in but then she didn't want to bother him. There was one thing that she knew; she didn't want this day to end.

Cheyenne was unsure how long she stood in front of the door before she finally took her room key out. She unlocked the door and walked in quietly, sitting the teas down softly on the bedside table. She slipped off her shoes and walked over the bed.

Carefully, she climbed in beside him. He was still sleeping on his side, facing the window. She slid under the blanket with him and put her hand on his naked chest. As she twirled his chest hair, he started to stir and rolled over onto his back. "Sebastian, wake up. I am bored." She kissed his ear. He just smiled at her without opening his eyes. "Honey, wake up with me, it's almost 9." She snuggled up to his chest as he put his arm around her.

"Maybe we should sleep all day," he said with his eyes still closed.

"Maybe, but I'm not tired. We should go do something. Or we can go back out to Marie's and get our stuff. I could use a shower."

He rolled over on top of her with no warning. "Or maybe we could just lay here all day," he said as he kissed her lips. It was a light, gentle kiss. Cheyenne rolled her eyes at him in a playful way. "Ok we can go and get our stuff and take a shower, he finally agreed"

He went to stand up and she grabbed his hands and pulled him back down to her. She cupped her hand behind his neck and leaned up to him for a kiss. This time his kiss was more powerful. He then suddenly pulled away from her. "We have to get going. I have to meet with Sarah today about my car."

Talk about a mood killer. "Yes, I remember," she said as he stood up and walked towards the bathroom. She tried as hard as she could to hide her hurt. She knew he was going to go back to her if they met and talked. He came out of the bathroom with a smile on his face. He seemed so happy today.

He looked over at her as if he could tell something was wrong. Then he came over and sat across the bed from her. "What's wrong, Honey?" He asked her as he put on his boxers. She didn't know if she should tell him or say nothing and force a smile on her face. She wasn't into lying. She hated when people lied to her.

"I just want to stay here forever. I don't want you to go talk to her. I know if you do..." She paused for a moment. "You won't come back. She will convince you to go back to her."

Sebastian got up from where he was sitting and walked over to where Cheyenne was sitting. "I cannot tell you what will become of us. But I can tell you that I won't desert you. We will figure it out. Ok?" He said as he cupped her chin and turned her face towards his. “I promise everything will be all right.” He lightly kissed her lips and then pulled away. “Are you hungry? Let’s go see what our friends are up to and get some food.” Sebastian added.

Cheyenne forced a smile on her face. “Well, we're waiting on you to get dressed, not me,” she said as playfully as she could. She had a sinking feeling in the pit of her stomach and was pretty sure she knew how this day was going to end.

When he finished dressing, they headed out to the car. She didn’t want to drive. “Sebastian, you drive,” she said as she headed over to the passenger side of the car. She got in and plugged in her phone because she knew it needed to be charged.

The ride to Marie’s was quiet. It was apparent that they both had things on their minds. She had no idea what he was thinking about, but she did have this odd feeling that today was going to be their last day together. She feared that once they both go back to work Monday, she would never see him again. She tried to shake the feeling, but for some reason it wouldn’t go away. Sebastian took his hand off the shifter and grabbed her hand, bringing it up to his lips, and kissed it.

“Honey, it will be ok. I promise you,” he said one last time as they pulled into Marie’s driveway.

“You can say that now, but I don’t think so. Once you go, I don't think you’ll come back,” she said as tears started to run down her face. He reached over and embraced her in a hug. He didn’t say anything. He just held her and let her cry. One hand was softly rubbing her back. When she finally got her crying under control, she pulled away from him. “Let’s just go inside and not ruin the day,” she suggested as she wiped her tears from her cheeks. She put on the best smile she could muster.

~~~~

They went inside and everyone was getting ready for the day. They all sat around and talked a while before Sebastian got up to walk outside. He was outside for a while before Cheyenne decided to go out and see what was wrong. She walked out the back door, and he was sitting on the deck staring at his phone. “What is the matter?” She asked him.
~~~~

He looked up at her. "Nothing really, just thinking."

"What are you thinking about?" She asked as she sat in the chair beside him.

"Nothing for you to worry about. I need to take a shower and then I have a few things I need to do today," Sebastian said.

"I'm sure you can take one here. I'll make sure there are towels in the bathroom," she said as she got up and turned to walk back inside the house. She knew he was acting weird, but there was nothing she could do. She made sure there were towels in the bathroom and then went back outside. "The bathroom is free."

"Thanks" was all he said and then went back to smoking his cigarette. Just as Cheyenne turned to head back inside, he spoke again. "You can take one first, if you want. I need to make a few more phone calls before I go in."

"All right, I will let you know when I'm done," she said as she went inside. She didn't give him time to say anything else. By the way he was acting, she knew that he was going back to Sarah. She didn't want to fight with what little time they had left together.

Cheyenne got her clothes and headed for the shower. She knew she had to take a bath because of the cast on her arm, but it would also give her some time to think. She had to figure out how to get him to stay. After she washed her body there was a knock at the door.

"It's me," said Marie from the other side of the door.

"Come in, I guess," Cheyenne said.

"So, what is going on between you two?" He seems upset. Did something happen?" Marie asked.

"The better question is what hasn't happened. We had an amazing night and today he's going to meet her. I know he won't be coming back to me. I think he feels it, and so do I."

"Well, you can't make him stay, Honey. I know you want to, but you can't. I say enjoy the time he is spending with you. It is his decision, and only he can make it. I don't think anything you say or do will change his decision. I know this isn't what you want to hear, but it is true," Marie said.

"I know, but it doesn't make it any easier. I care a lot for him, and all of this sucks. I feel like he cares for me, but I'm not sure," Cheyenne said as she struggled to hold back her tears.

"It will all turn out OK in the end, you will see. It may not be tomorrow or the next day... but someday it will, I promise you that much. Here, let me help you wash your hair so your cast doesn't get wet," Marie insisted, bending down over the tub to grab the shampoo.

After her hair was washed, she climbed out of the tub. Marie had left and then came back in a few minutes to help put her tresses into a loose messy bun. Cheyenne had picked out her black shirt T-shirt and blue-jean shorts. She took one last look in the mirror before heading out to tell Sebastian the shower was all his.

"Babe, the shower is all yours," she told him. He reached over and grabbed her hand.

"I'm coming. I'm not even sure where the bathroom is," he said with a wink. She glared at him with a seemingly exasperated grin.

"Well, maybe if you had used the bathroom last night instead of showering the poor tree, you would know where it is," she chided, pulling him up out of the chair. Sebastian embraced her in a hug. He didn't say anything, just hugged her. She waited a few minutes and then pulled away from him before she started to cry.

She didn't look at him. Instead, she just pulled him by the arm into the house. She escorted him to the bathroom and then went back outside to where Marie was sitting. She waited a little while for him to shower and then went back in to check on him.

She was walking in the dining room when he rounded the corner after emerging from the bathroom. Cheyenne walked over to him. "Hey," was all she said.

She wrapped her arms around his waist and rested her head on his chest. He wrapped his arms around her.

"Hey," he said.

"So... Do you want to take my car with you when you go talk to her?" She asked him.

"No, I'll take mine. Honey, you know you could have anyone one, like Paul, someone younger than me."

She knew where this conversation was going. She looked up at him. "That is not your choice, it is mine. Besides, I do what I want. You aren't the boss of me," she said as she kissed his freshly shaven face. She moved to his lips and kissed them gently.

"I know, Honey, I am just saying," he said. "Shall we head back outside?" He rested his head on her head. "I am going to head to town around noon. I have a few things that I need to do. Plus, I need to talk to her about keeping my car."

"OK" was the only response she could give. He held her for a few more minutes before he pulled away.

"Shall we go?" He asked.

"Yeah, probably, before they think we are being naughty in the house," she said with a chuckle. He smiled at her with his special smile, grabbed her hand, and they walked out back hand in hand. Before long, it was time for him to leave. She was starting to feel the pull; the emotional pull that was prying them apart. She really hoped it wasn't really what was about to happen, but she knew for sure that her time alone with him was coming to an end. Her time with him was coming to an end, period. They both sat on the bench on the north side of the deck.

"I apologize for last night. It was rude of me to get out of hand," Sebastian said.

"No worries, it was more Paul's fault than yours," Marie said. "I wanted to punch him myself."

"I still feel bad for being disrespectful to you guys in your own home. I should have kept myself under control." Sebastian added.

"Let's forget it and let it go," Cheyenne said. "There is no changing the past. There's no reason to dwell on it."

"Agreed," Marie said.

16

It had been a few hours since Sebastian left. She didn't want him to go, but he promised he would be back. Marie took her daughter upstairs to take a nap, so Cheyenne decided to lie down on the couch and rest for a while, too. She woke to the ringtone 'Addicted to.'

"Hello," she said.

"What are you doing, Honey?" Sebastian asked.

"I fell asleep on the couch. What's up?" Cheyenne asked him. She had a feeling he was calling to say he wasn't coming back.

"Ok, well, I am meeting her at 4 at the Lyons Park. If I don't message you or call you by 5:30, then go there," he said. Sebastian sounded distressed. "Remember, if I'm not there by 5:30, 6 at the latest."

"Yes, If I don't hear from you, I will go there."

"Don't forget," Sebastian added.

"I won't. Is everything ok?" She asked. He had her worried now.

"I hope so. Just remember. I've got to go, she just pulled up. Don't forget -5:30, Cheyenne. Say it back to me."

"I won't. If I don't hear from you by 5:30, 6 at the latest, I will go to Lyons Park." He didn't say goodbye or anything, he just hung up. When she looked up from the couch, Marie was in front of her.

"What is going on?" Marie asked. "Is he ok?"

"I don't know. He sounded seriously distressed," Cheyenne answered. She looked at her phone to see what time it was. It was only 4:03. This may be the longest hour and half of her life. "Well, want to go get stuff to cook for dinner? I can cook if you want…" Cheyenne didn't even get to finish her sentence before Marie interrupted her.

"Umm, NO! I don't want to die. Honey… Your cooking sucks. Please don't torture me today," Marie said as she stepped back away from Cheyenne. She was trying not to start laughing.

"Hey, I can cook something," Cheyenne retorted.

"Like what, fast food?" Marie asked as she took off towards the kitchen.

Cheyenne yelled behind her "Ha, ha. You're such a funny woman." Cheyenne laid back on the couch. *What could possibly be going on that has Sebastian acting so strange? Come to think of it, he had been acting that way all day.*

"Come outside, Cheyenne. We are going to start the grill," Marie yelled from the other room.

Cheyenne rolled her eyes. "I'll be right there." She kind of wanted to go back to sleep. She was tired. She had not been getting much sleep since she and Marie stayed up drinking the last couple nights. She was starting to regret their choices. With a huff, Cheyenne finally got up and went outside.

It wasn't long after she went outside that Sebastian called back. "Hello," she answered, scared to death of what he was going to say on the other end of the phone.

"Yo!" He said with a small giggle. He knew what the word 'yo' meant to her. "What are you doing?"

"Still sitting here at Marie's."

"Are you staying around again tonight?" Sebastian asked.

"I can. I can stay here or get a room if you would like?"

"Yeah. Can you get us a room?" He asked in a pleading tone.

"Sure, where would you like me to get it?" Cheyenne asked.

"The one by my work. Please."

"Yep, I can call there. I'll let you know if they have a room," she said. "I'll call you back. Are you heading here now?"

"No, not yet. I'm going to drive around for a while. I'll let you know when I head up there."

"Ok, I'll talk to you later. Bye," she replied.

"Bye," he said. She leaned back on the bench.

Cheyenne had no idea what happened. She wanted to ask, but she didn't want to pry. She called the hotel. They did have a room. She let them know that a friend might pick up her keys and gave them his name.

She sent Sebastian a text. "Can you pick up the keys from the Comfort Inn? I told them your name and said you might pick them up."

"Yeah, I can pick them up. I'll head up there in about an hour."

It was about a half hour later when he messaged her again.

"Taylor, right?"

"Yes." She sent back to him in a message. She couldn't believe that he couldn't remember her last name, even though she had told him it was Taylor many times.

"Ask if he's eating supper with us. It will be ready at about 6:30," Marie said as she looked up from the blanket she was lying on. She was trying to tan. "And move, please, you're blocking my sun. Either lie back down or something."

"I'm going to stay right here and make you have my handprint in your tan line. I'll text him, give me a minute," Cheyenne said as she rolled her eyes.

"Did you just roll your eyes at me?"

"Yep, I sure did. Here, I'll do it again," she said, rolling her eyes at her once again. They both started to giggle. Cheyenne grabbed her phone from her pocket, flopped back on the ground and clicked on Sebastian's name to start a text to him.

"Are you going to eat dinner with us? Marie is making bacon-wrapped chicken, potatoes and asparagus."

"Sure, what time?" He replied.

"She says it will be ready around 6:30," Cheyenne wrote.

"All right, I might be a little late. See you soon," Sebastian answered.

She laid back on the blanket. "He said he will be here, though he may be a little late." Cheyenne said, turning her head towards Marie.

"Good," Marie answered, cracking a smile.

"I'm not sure what you're trying to do," Cheyenne said, turning her head back towards the sky.

"I'm not trying to do anything. I just asked if he was coming to dinner, that's all." Marie said.

~~~~

Marie was just starting to make up the plates when Sebastian showed up to the house. They all sat at the table, Sebastian on the end and Cheyenne to his left. Marie sat to the left of Cheyenne. Marie's boyfriend, Terry, wasn't hungry, so he didn't eat. Cheyenne ate most of the chicken and half of the potato, foregoing the asparagus.

Sebastian, using his fork, stabbed the asparagus on her plate. "Eat your greens."

"Nope, I'm good." Cheyenne said.

"Yes, you need to eat them or at least try them," he said as he took a piece of her asparagus and flung it into his mouth.

"Well, if you think it's so yummy, you eat it," she said.

"Fine, I will." Sebastian said as he picked up another piece and started to eat it. He offered her a bite, but she scrunched up her nose and turned her face away from him. "You need to eat the rest of your chicken."

"No, I don't. I've eaten all I can eat," she insisted with a bit of attitude. He didn't say anything, just stared at her. She stared back at him until she broke into a grin. then in a few seconds, so did he.

Cheyenne stood up and took her plate to the kitchen, scraped and rinsed it. She came back and grabbed Sebastian's. He thanked her as she carried it to the kitchen.

Sebastian went outside with Terry. They both had a beer in their hand. Marie started the dishes while Cheyenne helped clean up. "Well, that was a nice dinner. Thank you, Marie, for inviting Sebastian. He promised me a long time ago that we would have dinner together. I expected to go out to dinner with him, but this worked too."

"Yes, it was nice. I just about lost it when he was bossing you about eating your asparagus. You should have said 'Yes, Daddy.' That would have been funny," Marie said, trying to control her giggles.
~~~~

"I never think of a good comeback until it is done and over with. Dang it," Cheyenne said as she started laughing.

Suddenly they turned around to a voice. "What are you two laughing about?" Sebastian asked. Terry and Sebastian were standing in the doorway of the back porch.

The two girls looked at each other and started laughing harder. "Nothing," Marie finally managed to spit out.

"I don't think they are going to tell us their inside joke," Terry said to Sebastian.

"You're probably right," Sebastian said as they each grabbed another beer and headed back outside.

After the girls finished cleaning up from supper, they went outside with the guys. Sebastian was playing ball with Marie's daughter. It was more like he was a dog fetching the ball. She would throw it towards him and miss, and he would go get it and roll it back to her.

It was very cute to see how well he played with kids. Cheyenne wondered if he was ever like that with his children. From what she understood, he hadn't seen two of his kids since they were very young. And his daughter, who lived nearby, he wasn't in her life much. She was told it was because his girlfriend and his ex-wife had a falling out. Cheyenne could see that with the way Sebastian's girlfriend acted most days. In her opinion, she acted like a child.

When they walked out the door Sebastian looked up at Cheyenne and smiled. She loved his special smile. She flashed a small smile back. The last 24 hours have been great. Seeing Sebastian free from the stressful life that he lived made her happy. She really hoped he didn't go back to her and back to that life. He was a different person when she was around.

She wasn't sure how long they had been sitting there talking when he finally said, "Honey, we should be going, it's almost 8:30."

"You are right, we probably should be going." They said their goodbyes and walked to their cars.

"I'm going to stop at the gas station and then I'll meet you there. I need cigarettes and some tea. Here's a room key for you," Sebastian said handing her the key.

"OK," she said as she got in her car and headed out of town. As she drove to the hotel, she couldn't shut off her brain. She knew something was missing, and her gut told her that her whole world was about to change. Cheyenne grabbed her overnight bag and headed into the hotel and waited for Sebastian to show up.

Soon it was 10 p.m. She finally got tired of waiting for him and went to text him, but before she could type in what she wanted to say, she received a text from him.

"Be there shortly... talking to the wife." She hated when he called her his wife; they weren't even married.

"K, did you go there?" She asked him.

"No, was talking on the phone." Then he added, "10 min."

The next thing she knew, her phone was ringing his ringtone. 'Hello," she answered.

"The side door is locked and the key won't work. Can you come let me in?" Sebastian asked her.

"Yeah, I'll be right there." She slipped her shoes on and headed down the hall to the door. She could see him standing there looking so handsome. She was wishing she could just stop time. She opened the door, and he followed her down to the room.

"Why are all the lights off?" He asked her.

"I was stretching on the floor and thinking, listening to my music. I figured you changed your mind," she said as he flipped on one of the lights. She sat down on the queen-sized bed she got for them to share. She sat facing the window, struggling to hold in her tears. She knew from his demeanor that he was leaving her.

"Honey, you're going to be mad at me," he said as he stood in front of her. He crouched down in front of her, placing his hands on her legs.

"You're going back to her. Why?" She asked.

"Six years is a long time to throw away. Are you mad at me?"

"No, I'm not mad. Are you leaving now to go?"

"No. I told her I would come home after work tomorrow."

"Oh," was all Cheyenne could say. She didn't know what else to say. She knew he was never going to be hers, no matter what she did.

"Hey, look at me." She looked up at him. "Let's not ruin the night. If you want me to leave, I can, but I would like to stay here with you. It is your choice."

"I want you to stay. Can we talk about something else?" She asked him. He stood up and flopped down on the end of the bed.

"Sure, what do you want to talk about, your bad taste in relaxing music?" He asked with a playful smile. She laughed at him.

17

They sat and talked until about 11:30, knowing they both had to work in the morning.

Cheyenne climbed under the blanket fully clothed. "Are you sleeping with your clothes on?" He asked her.

"I was going to. Didn't figure you wanted to sleep with me naked anymore."

"Oh, Honey... I didn't say that."

"Pretty much you did. You chose her over me, so, I figured you wouldn't want to be naked with me."

"I didn't say that. I know all this doesn't make sense, but I promise I will explain it all later. Lay with me naked, please." He said, his voice almost pleading.

"Ok," she as she slid her tank top over her head. Then she slipped off her shorts while staying under the blanket. She watched as Sebastian stood by the side of the bed and pulled his blue Under Armour shirt off over his head, dropping it on the floor. He turned towards the bed to slip off his shoes. He looked Cheyenne in the eyes as he unbuttoned his shorts and let them fall to the floor. She could see his erect cock poking through his boxers.

She started to chew on her lower lip as she watched him slowly slide his boxers down his legs, never letting his eyes leave hers. Cheyenne could stare at his naked body all day. However, he didn't give her much time to look.

He crawled in bed beside her and laid down on his back with the blankets pulled up to his chest. She didn't know what to do or how to act now that she had acquired the new knowledge that he was returning to his girlfriend, so she rolled away from him, on to her side.

Sebastian climbed up beside her, and with his body against hers, lightly kissed her shoulder. He slightly moved her hair off her neck and began kissing a trail leading up to her neck. She moaned and rolled over onto her back. Sebastian climbed on top of Cheyenne. When their eyes locked, he smiled and tilted his head down to kiss her lips.

Cheyenne lifted her hand, rubbing it on his face. He pressed his cheek into her palm and closed his eyes for just a moment. Cheyenne didn't want this moment to end. She wished there was a way they could be together. She was lost in her thoughts when he spoke. "We don't have to do this, if you don't want to." He leaned down to kiss her again. Cheyenne turned her head away from him.

"I want to, but I get to be in control," she uttered as she pushed him off her. He rolled over the rest of the way, which helped because there was no way she could move him off her all by herself. She climbed on top of him, slowly sliding his cock inside of her. She didn't move, just sat there and smiled. She leaned down and kissed him, nibbling on his bottom lip as she grabbed his hands with hers. She settled his hands on top of her thighs, placing her hands on his chest to slowly lifted herself up and down on him.

"Mmm," Sebastian moaned. He lifted his hands to her waist as if to lift her. She stopped his hands midair. This time she settled them on her breasts. Cheyenne started to move faster and faster. Sebastian's moans started to get louder. She loved the control she had. She could stop at any moment and there was nothing he could do. Finally, she had some sort of control over him.

She started to slow her movement down again. She loved teasing him, but apparently Sebastian had a different idea. He reached his arms up and wrapped them around her. He pulled her down so that they were chest to chest. And then suddenly, he rolled them over, still staying inside her.

Sebastian pinned her hands down. "My turn, Love." He kissed her neck and all over her chest as he moved his body.

Cheyenne gasped at the enjoyment she was feeling. He never ceased to amaze her. Her body was on sensory overload. She tried to move her hands, but he had them clasped within his hands and pinned to the bed. She tried once again to pull them away. She wanted to touch his body, but she couldn't move. The faster Sebastian moved, the harder he held her down.

Then suddenly, he just stopped. She knew he wasn't finished. "Why did you stop?" Cheyenne asked in a near whine as he let her hands free.

"I want you to stand up and bend over," he said flatly as he stood beside the bed.

She rolled over to the side of the bed and stood up as he insisted, but instead of bending over, she walked around him. He spun around, following her movement. She reached up and pushed him onto the bed. His legs were hanging off the edge. She knelt between them and grabbed his cock with her good hand. He started to sit up as if attempting to stop her, but she quickly proceeded to lick his shaft. He fell back onto the bed and moaned profusely. She deep-throated him, sliding his hardness as far down as she could. While caressing the area between his balls and his cock, she slowly slid her mouth up the shaft, keeping her lips tight around him, and then she sucked him as hard as she could manage. He moaned and twisted with each movement as she moved his cock in and out of her mouth while continuing to rub his balls, sometimes tracing the edges with her index finger. "Oh, my God! Cheyenne, stop, or I'm going to cum!" She didn't stop. Instead, she moved faster and faster, until she finally felt him explode in her mouth like a champaign bottle blowing its cork. She swallowed it down and looked up at him, wiping her lips with the back of her hand, almost proud of her ability to render him listless. By now he was in a sitting position.

"And you say you have no experience. I strongly disagree." He pulled her up on the bed to lay on top of him. He kissed her a few times before she climbed off him and over to her side of the bed.

She laid beside him with her head on his chest, his right arm around her. Having him hold her felt amazing. Cheyenne felt so safe in his arms. "Honey, I have a question for you," she said as she snuggled his chest more.

"Yes," he said, brushing the hair from her face. She looked up at him.

"Why can't we continue this? I mean, why does she have to know? Why do we have to stop?"

"It just has to for now," he said. She didn't know what to say. He lightly rubbed her back.

"Maybe I should just go then," she said as she started to get up.

He grabbed her with the arm he had around her and put his legs over hers. "Please stay!"

"Why? Why do you even want me here?" She asked.

"Because I don't want you to leave me. Promise me you will stay."

She relaxed in his arms. "I promise to stay," she said as the tears ran down her face.

"Baby don't cry. I promise it will all turn out," Sebastian told her as he held her in his arms. He held her until she drifted off into a deep sleep.

~~~~

Cheyenne woke to her alarm. She rolled over to where Sebastian had been the night before. He was gone. She sat up and started to panic. As she was about to get out of bed to see if his car was gone, he rounded the corner from the bathroom. "You're awake early," he said as he slid back into bed beside her.

"My alarm just went off," she said, glancing at the clock on the wall. It was 5:30 a.m. She sighed. She must not have changed the alarm to 6:30. It was way too early to get up.

"I'm sorry if I startled you. I had to go to the bathroom. We don't have to get up just yet. We can go back to sleep or just lay here together. I think we should lay here," he said.

She didn't answer him, she just rolled over and snuggled up to him. He kissed her forehead. "Sebastian, how are we going to do this now?"

"What do you mean?" He asked as he rubbed her shoulder with his thumb.

"Are we putting an end to us completely, or what?" Cheyenne was pretty sure she didn't want to know the answer.
~~~~

"For now, we need to end the sex," he said.

"I can still text you?" She asked him as she looked up to him.

"Yes, but just the other phone. Ok?" He kissed her forehead again. She wasn't sure this was going to work this way. She didn't know if she could just stop. How was she going to walk away from her happiness?

"I guess." *Why couldn't they just continue what they were doing? It wasn't like his girlfriend knew what was going on.* She just laid on his chest. Neither one of them spoke. She really didn't have anything to say to him. It was more like she didn't know what to say.

Cheyenne wasn't sure if she had drifted off to sleep, because the next thing she knew, his alarm was going off, letting them know it was time to face the world. She stretched and rolled out of bed. Sebastian was already awake, sitting on the side of the bed watching her. "Good morning," he said.

"Morning. I don't know about good, but it's morning," she replied. She was unsure why he was watching her. "How long have you been awake?"

"I never went back to sleep." Sebastian was sitting up with his back against the headboard. She couldn't tell if he was still naked or if he had slipped on his boxers. He had the sheet pulled up covering his lower body. "Come here for a moment," he said as he patted the bed beside him.

She stood there naked by the bed for a moment staring at him. He patted the bed again. She crawled up beside him, and Sebastian pulled the sheet over them. He wrapped his right arm around her, pulling her close to him. "Don't you have to go to work?" She asked.

"Yeah, but I want to hold you for a moment. I have something that I need to talk to you about." He stopped talking and cupped her chin with his other hand, slowly pulling her face up to his. He lightly kissed it. "Cheyenne, I'm leaving in two days. I put in my notice at work. I am leaving to go back home. Back to South Carolina. I decided to do it last night, after we talked."

"Why are you leaving? What about your girlfriend?" Cheyenne asked, struggling to hold back her tears.

"Honey, I need a reset in my life. I'm going to tell her she can come with me if she wants. My transfer was accepted. I had been thinking about it for a while." She started to cry. He pulled her in tightly and hugged her. In doing that he made her cry even more. "I have no reason to stay here."

"You have reasons. You have me! You know I care about your dumb ass for some odd reason," she said almost in a scream as she pushed away from him. "Doesn't that matter to you at all? Does it not matter that I care and don't want you to leave?"

"Cheyenne, I need a new start. I know you don't understand, but I do. I don't want to fight with you. We will talk about this more later. We have to get ready for work," he said as he got up and headed to the bathroom. She watched his naked body walk away from her. He just left her sitting on the bed, alone. She had no idea what had happened after she fell asleep. Did he fight with her more?

The rest of the morning was quiet; neither spoke until it was time to leave. "Sebastian," she said.

"Yeah?"

"Can we just agree to disagree?" She knew saying these words meant neither won the fight or disagreement. It meant they would drop it and resume it later.

"Agreed," he said with a smile. He embraced her in a hug and held her for a moment. Then he engaged her in a passionate kiss. "Honey, I have to go, I'm already late. I'll text you." He gave her one last kiss on the forehead. It was probably the last kiss she would ever get. Then he walked out of the room, leaving her standing there.

Cheyenne got ready, grabbed her work stuff, and headed to the shop.

18

Cheyenne pulled into the shop, but before she went inside, she sent Sebastian a text. "Are you having a good morning at work?"

"Too early to tell... I am tired," he replied.

"I'm sorry you're tired. Hopefully it's a good day for you. So, question for you. What would you like me to do to make your life less complicated, since I am the one who complicated it?" She asked, before going on in to work.

"It has nothing to do with you."

"Then what does it have to do with?" She waited a few seconds before texting again. "Never mind, I shouldn't pry into your business. If you want to talk about it, I'm here to talk."

His answer was quick. "I really am going to move."

"Why move and what about your girlfriend?"

"What about her?" He answered.

"If you're going to move, are you going to ask her to go with you? Or are you just walking away from everyone and everything?" She was starting to become angry with him.

"Just me and a bag of clothes... That's the way I have always done it."

Cheyenne took a deep breath before she answered him this time. She was about to lose her patience with him. "So, you're running then? Why?"

"Walking," Sebastian said. Some days he acted like a child, and it drove her crazy.

"Whatever! Why? I'd like to know an honest answer." She was now beyond angry with him. She was beginning to think he was trying to make her mad at him to make it easier for him to walk away from her.

"Just time to reset my life."

Cheyenne thought for a moment before she started to type. "This is coming from someone who says he's too old to start over.... I call BS. You have do have reasons. But if you don't want to tell me.... That is your choice. I won't push you, but I don't feel like it's fair for you to walk(run) from everyone in your life. I'm not going to fight with you on it. It's your life, your choices, even though I disagree. Besides, my opinion means very little to you anyway. You can say it has nothing to do with me, but I don't believe you. You told me your life was simple till I fucked that up. I cannot undo that."

His answer startled her. "OK."

"That's it?" She asked.

"Yep," he replied.

"Why? Are you mad?" She asked.

"Nope," he answered.

"So, why are you afraid to talk to me about serious things?"

Sebastian's next message made her blood start to boil. "I'm not, and I'm not going to argue with you. I am a big boy and don't have to rationalize anything to anyone. I'm leaving in two days."

"And I get that. I'm trying to be a friend and talk to you about what's going on with you, not rationalize. I know you'll do what you want, cuz you're a stubborn ass. I was just trying to help you. You know damn well I care about you, sooo we will go this route.... Then fine, how about this one... I'll be selfish, I don't want you to move away. I don't want to lose my friend. I struggle not talking to you for 24 hours. I couldn't imagine not talking to you at all. Yes, I'm thinking of my feelings, not yours." She waited a few hours and when she didn't get a reply, she texted him again. "Well, I guess I have nothing left to say..."

"I doubt that," he replied within seconds.

"Nope, I don't." She knew she wouldn't get an answer this time. She messed up. She finished out the day and went back to her hotel room.

~~~~
~~~~

The next morning, she thought about texting that she was sorry, but she couldn't bring herself to swallow her pride. Cheyenne didn't feel like working. She called in to her dad and told him she wasn't feeling well. Thankfully he didn't need her. She just laid in the bed and cried and slept. She wanted to talk to him so badly. He was leaving sometime in the morning, and she had no idea what to say. What could she say to make him see how much she loved him and needed him? For the next 24 hours all she did was pace the room, sleep and cry. When morning came, she knew it was too late. Too late to tell him what she wanted to say.

She stood there looking out the window of the hotel room. She was unsure how long she had been standing there staring through the glass. She had a perfect view of where he once worked; a perfect view of where his car once sat, but he was no longer there, no longer in her life. He warned her that he was leaving, though he called it, "walking away to reset his life." She wasn't sure how she was going to make it and go on with her own life. How was she going to live without him in it? He was the beat to her heart. Sebastian was more than a lover; he was a close friend. He told her that he was leaving two days before he did. She had two days to talk him into staying, but all she could manage to say to him was, "You know damn well I care for you, sooo." But he never replied. *Why didn't she just tell him that she loved him? Why was she so stupid?*

Instead of using her last text to talk to him and say, "Hey, I love you," she texts him back to say, "I've got nothing left to say."

He replied to her quickly, making her heart beat faster in hopes he would say that he didn't want to leave, but instead he replied with, "I doubt that."

"Nope, I don't...." She replied to him.

Why didn't she have the guts to say how she really felt about him? Maybe if she would have told him that she loved him he would have stayed. She squeezed her eyes shut one last time to hold back her tears and took a deep breath. She looked out over the parking lot one more time and pictured his car still there. With a sigh, she reached down and picked up her phone as the last words of *Here Without You* played...... *But you're still with me in my dreams. And tonight, girl it's only you and me.* Cheyenne, with her bags in hand, walked to the hotel room door and paused for a moment, turning around to take one last look around the room they once shared. With that, she took a deep breath and headed to her car. Cheyenne sat in her Jeep for some time, staring at his parking space just a couple hundred feet in front of her. Closing her eyes, she imagined his smile as he stood beside his car. That memory was all she had left of him. These are her memories that would never fade.

19

Epilogue

It had been two years since she last saw him; two years since he walked out of her life and the life of the child she carried. There were many times she thought about messaging him on Facebook, but she had no idea what to say to him, or if he would even get the message.

Her son looked just like him. There was no denying who his father was. So far, his personality was just like his. It took a while for her dad to come to peace with what had happened between her and Sebastian. He was angrier with him than he was with her. It was a warm spring day. She hadn't been at work very long when the door opened and closed. She looked up from the paperwork in front of her. She was not expecting to see the man who was standing in front of her.

Her eyes widened with shock, and she felt almost frozen in time. "Hey, Sweetheart. Wow, this place has really changed in the last two years!" He scanned around the room, and Cheyenne followed his eyes, which landed on the picture of her and her children on the wall behind her.

"What are you doing here?" She asked, still in shock that he was standing in front of her.

He just stood there staring at the picture on the wall. Slowly, he walked over and stood in front of it. In the image Cheyenne was holding a little boy. He was almost 9 months old in the photo, with dark-brown hair and blue eyes. He had the same facial structure as Sebastian. Beside her stood her other son. The two boys did not look the same, yet they resembled each other.

"He's mine, isn't he?" Sebastian asked with a small quiver in his voice.

Cheyenne ignored his question. "Sebastian, what are you doing here?"

He turned and looked squarely at her; all the color was gone from his face. "I just transferred back. I had a few things that I needed to take care of up here. Answer the question, Cheyenne, is he mine?"

"No! He's not yours. What would give you that idea?"

"I've heard things. You know that people talk."

Cheyenne just stared at him for a moment. "I don't care what you have heard. I honestly don't care."

"Why do you feel you need to lie to me?" Sebastian asked, still speaking in a calm voice.

"I'm not lying to you! You need to leave, Sebastian. I don't want you here or around me!"

"Fine, but this conversation isn't over! I want the truth, Cheyenne. Don't make me take actions to get the answers I need."

"Are you threatening me?"

"Not at all. If he is my son, I will be part of his life. There is nothing you can do to stop me," he said in a firm tone. "You need to tell me the truth now."

"Sebastian, you need to leave."

Before Cheyenne knew what was happening, Sebastain took four long strides towards her. He reached around her neck, slowly pulling her close to him. Her knees began to quiver. She wanted this so badly, but she knew she should be telling him no. Before she could stop it, he was kissing her, and all she could do was let her body melt with his. His kiss didn't last very long before he pulled away. "You will be hearing from my attorney," Sebastian said as he turned and walked out the front door.

To be continued......

About the Author

Katrena Gillis is the mother of three amazing children. Her children and her own love for reading have inspired her to write. Katrena wants to help readers to be able to travel to a new world and light up at new ideas as the stories come to life in their minds.

When she was young, she endured several difficult situations. When her mother became seriously ill and later when her best friend died in a car accident. It was during these tough times that Katrena fell deep into reading and began writing her own stories.

www.ingramcontent.com/pod-product-compliance
Lightning Source LLC
Chambersburg PA
CBHW070626310726
48982CB00001B/182

* 9 7 8 1 7 3 3 2 3 0 2 5 4 *